BOOK ONE

Lust for Living Press is an imprint of
COURAGE CRAFTERS, INC.

Copyright © 2018 by Richard Fenton & Andrea Waltz.
All rights reserved.

ISBN 978-1-947814-00-4

DISCLAIMER:
This book is a work of fiction. And while some real locations, historical
events, company names and easily recognizable public figures have been
used, the story is strictly the product of the authors' imaginations.
Beyond that, any names and/or resemblance to actual persons, living or
dead, is purely coincidental.

GET ENTANGLED

Visit Our Webb-Page

www.OnyxWebb.com

ONYX WEBB
Self-Portrait, Pencil on Paper
1941

FROM THE JOURNAL OF ONYX WEBB

I want to be alive again, feel wind blow through my hair.
Take a deep, glorious breath, have my lungs fill up with air.
I even want to feel the pain as thorns draw drops of blood.
Run outside in a pouring rain, dance barefoot in the mud.

What good is hearing music when you cannot sense the beat?
What purpose does passion serve for a soul that feels no heat?
Why pray for more tomorrows when your present is such hell?
Why hope to one day fall in love if you have no heart to swell?

There was a time when I believed that I would do it all—
Climb the Eiffel Tower; walk China's long Great Wall.
Dance on my wedding night, in the arms of the perfect man,
But life did not turn out that way, for fate had other plans.

What good is one more day on Earth? I ask myself again.
I know that I was happy once, yet cannot remember when.
Why continue on this way, doing nothing but survive?
Why stay among the living, simply dying to be alive?

-Onyx Webb
Crimson Cove, Oregon

Message from the Authors

First, a confession. We did not write this book—not alone, at least. We had an enormous amount of help from a ghostwriter.

Her name is *Onyx Webb*.

Joking aside, there were many times when it felt like the series was writing itself, with us simply typing as fast as we could to capture what was being *channeled* through us. And, at the risk of appearing mentally unbalanced, we can honestly tell you that every character has become a friend.

- *We've eaten our meals with them—breakfast, lunch and dinner—for over two years now...*
- *We understand what they want, who they love, what they fear and how they've been hurt...*
- *They show up in our dreams and tell us things most people would never share with another human being...*
- *Even the most-evil of our characters have grown on us—once we got to know them, that is.*

We don't expect you to understand. Not yet at least. But by the end of the series, you will.

In any case, don't pass judgment on any of the characters too soon, for—as in life—the people we trust most will disappoint us sometimes, while those we expect nothing from will surprise us with their courage and their humanity.

To be sure, Onyx Webb is not your run-of-the-mill, small-cast, chronological book series. It's a multi-layered, zig-zag, roller coaster ride, with enough twists and turns to keep you engaged and guessing to the very end.

Richard Fenton & Andrea Waltz
(writing as Diandra Archer)

Episode 1
The Story Begins

This Episode Dedicated to:

Ryan Murphy & Brad Falchuk

Every show you have ever created should be watched, studied, and dissected by any storyteller with a desire to thrill and entertain their fans.

And to the following
Onyx Webb "Super Fans"...

Glenda Pribus
Kelly Hill
Gene Smith & Kim Myers

Without your support, Onyx would cease to exist.

Written primarily to music by:

30 Seconds to Mars

In particular...

"Closer to the Edge"
"Up in the Air"
"Kings and Queens"
"The Kill"
"Do or Die"
"Search and Destroy"

NEAR ST. LOUIS, MISSOURI
AUGUST 5, 1904

Every train car was packed, every seat taken, with still more people standing in the aisles. Onyx was wide awake with anticipation, the excitement of the fair coursing through her veins like electricity. She reached up and tapped her father on the shoulder, but the big man was sound asleep. Onyx reached up and poked her father again, harder this time until Catfish opened his eyes and smiled.

"When do we get there, Papa? Are we close?" Onyx asked.

Catfish Webb gazed out the window of the train and could see the pale shades of sunrise—pink and yellow and orange—painted on the horizon. "Soon, child, soon," the burly French Cajun muttered. "Now close your eyes and..."

"Tell me again about how you and Mama met," Onyx said.

"I told you all 'dis already, Jitterbug."

"I know," said Onyx, "but tell it again! Please?" There it was, the one word Catfish was powerless against, and they both knew it: *please.*

"Very well, child, if it is a story you want, a story you shall have," Catfish said. He shifted in his seat and looked down at Onyx, her eyes wide and waiting. "Your daddy was out in the swamps, ten miles or more. I finished setting my traps and was lookin' for a patch of dry ground on which to sleep..."

"And then you saw the light, right?" Onyx interrupted.

"Who tellin' this story, you or me?" Catfish asked. Onyx moved her thumb and forefinger across her lips as if zipping them shut and holding back a giggle until Catfish continued.

"Very well, then. As I was about to say, your daddy saw a light through the trees, off in the distance, and I went to see who was goin' there. When I got closer, I saw it was a band of 'travelers,' what people call Gypsies. They were singin' and dancin' up a storm, and in the middle of 'em all, there stood the most beautiful sight I'd ever seen."

"It was Mama, right?" Onyx said softly.

Catfish nodded, lost for a moment in the memory. "Yes, it was Jofranka, your mama. And she saw me, too—looked right at me even though I was a hundred yards away peeking through the trees. She waved her hand as if invitin' me to join them, which your daddy surely did. They were nice to me, fed me up a nice supper, and let me stay for the night."

"And then..." Onyx prompted.

"And then the next morning I asked your mama if she might want to take a walk with your daddy..."

"Like a first date?" Onyx asked.

"Yes, child, like a date. We walked and talked for what must have been that entire day, 'cause the next thing I know it's nighttime again. We did this every day for almost a week, singin' and dancin' and walkin' and talkin' and then I just did it..."

"You asked her to marry you, then and there," Onyx said, finishing the sentence.

"Yes I did, Jitterbug. When you find the one, you just know. She said yes, so long as I could get permission from Loiza, the 'King of the Gypsies.' Without this man's permission, she could not leave the band. So I made him an offer..."

"You gave him your catfish traps, right?"

"Yes, each and every one, 'cause you can always get more fishin' traps, but you can't always find yourself another perfect woman. And that's how your mama and I became man and wife."

"And then I was born and Mama picked my name and called me Onyx, right?"

"Yes, the name *Onyx* was your mama's choice."

"But you call me Jitterbug because I'm always moving around and never standing still, not even for a second."

"Yep, child, you are just like a jitterbug lure, dancing and gleamin' in the water, doing everything you can to attract attention, just like now."

"Tell me again where Mama is now. Up in heaven, right?"

"Yes, Onyx, Mama is up in heaven..."

"Singing songs and waiting for us to join her, right?" Onyx asked.

"That's right, singing songs and dancing around in circles, making big giant swirls in the clouds," he said, turning his head to look out the window, the sky now filled with dark shades of red and orange and wisps of pale blue. "Now get some rest, child. We be in St. Louis soon enough, and we gonna need all the energy we can muster, so many wonderful things to see, so many things they got to do up there."

"Tell me a ghost story, papa, and I promise I'll go to sleep," Onyx said curling into a ball on the wooden bench and placing her head in his lap.

"Very well," Catfish began: *"It was a dark and stormy night..."*

"No, the other one," Onyx said.

"You want the scary one?" Catfish asked in mock surprise. "Are you sure?"

"Yes! Tell the one where the woman is being chased in the woods by the wolves!" Onyx said. "I won't have bad dreams, I promise."

Catfish nodded and began again: *"It was late at night and the moon was full, with wolf bane hanging from the trees, when off in the distance the woman could hear the howling of wolves..."*

Catfish looked down and saw that his young daughter was already fast asleep, which was a good thing since Catfish had no earthly idea how the story ended—they'd never gotten that far. He ran his fingers gently through his daughter's hair and wondered where Onyx's mother really was.

He hated lying to her, but there were some things he simply couldn't tell the child.

Not yet, at least.

*   *   *

Catfish hadn't closed his eyes for more than a minute when the dream began.

Jofranka is lying in bed—her pregnant belly rising and falling with each labored breath—her skin gray, the color of ash. "We knew this was possible, André," she says. "Loiza warned us."

"No," Catfish says, his voice pleading. "You can do this, you hear me? You are gonna be just fine, the baby gonna be fine..."

"Onyx," Jofranka says.

"What?"

"Onyx—that should be her name," Jofranka says. "I want you to name her Onyx."

"We're having a baby girl?" Catfish asks. "Our baby is going to be a girl?"

Jofranka nods then gasps in excruciating pain, becoming so transparent now that Catfish could almost see right through her.

"Tell her how badly I wanted her," Jofranka manages through gritted teeth. "Tell her that I loved her... make sure you tell her... make sure..."

"What can I do?" Catfish pleads. "Tell me, Jo. There must be something—"

"Give her my red keepsake box... when she's old enough to understand. And tell her she is not to have a child, André!"

"No, no, you gonna be here. You can tell her..."

"Promise me," Jofranka manages when the contraction subsides. "Promise me."

Catfish nods, tears streaming down his face as he accepts the truth—he is about to lose his wife, and there is nothing he can do to stop it.

Jofranka cries out as the next contraction begins. "This is it, Jofranka, you can do this," he says. "You do this, okay? You push hard as you can and it will be done, just this one last time."

Catfish could see the baby now, making its way out of Jofranka toward him. He reached down, placed his hand beneath Onyx's head. "Push, Jo! Push!"

Jofranka's final scream is ear-piercing, animal-like, as Onyx emerges into the safety of Catfish's large hands. "My God, she's so beautiful, a girl like you said. Look, Jo, at what you have done!"

Catfish lifts Onyx for his wife to see. But she is no longer there, having transferred what little energy she had left to produce her child.

Then Catfish awoke as he always did.

His face wet with tears.

BURBANK, CALIFORNIA
DECEMBER 23, 1971

Juniper Cole should have been nervous. After all, it wasn't every day that someone got to go on the Johnny Carson show.

But, being only eight years old, she didn't fully grasp the importance of the situation. Besides, she had the greatest shield any young girl could ask for—she had Quinn.

"Don't worry, June, you're gonna be great," Quinn told her. And if Quinn said she was going to be great, then she would be.

Quinn was Juniper's protector.

And it didn't matter that he was only twelve years old. As far as Juniper Cole was concerned, Quinn was God. And like God, Quinn was always there. Unfortunately, the same couldn't be said for her parents.

Quinn stood by Juniper's side as Mr. Carson introduced her to the studio audience, referring to her as a "child prodigy," whatever that meant.

The only thing Juniper knew was that she liked to play. She loved the vibration of the notes as they rose from the giant instrument and filled the room with sound, and marveled at how her fingers somehow knew where to go next as they danced across the ivory keys.

When the red curtain pulled back, Juniper made her way across the stage to thunderous applause, which still confused her since she hadn't done anything yet. She took her seat at the large grand piano, then smiled and waved as she'd been taught to do since her first public performance at the age of three.

Juniper counted to five in her head, allowing the room to go completely silent, then ran through her checklist:

Make two tight fists...

Open fingers and stretch them out...

Relax fingers completely...

Place fingers on keys in starting position...
Form a dome with fingers curved...
Breathe in...
Breathe out...
Be magnificent.

LONDON, ENGLAND
JANUARY 10, 2010

The size of the crowd outside the BBC Broadcasting House, in the heart of London, would have made most people think the Pope was visiting. But the gender of the crowd (at least 95 percent were female) and the average age (somewhere south of 25) told another story.

A line of London police officers did their best to maintain order, but when a white Mercedes Benz stretch limousine approached and pulled to a stop at the curb, all hell broke loose. The crowd surged toward the limo, and when the rear door swung open and a gray-haired BBC executive emerged, the group groaned.

They did not know that the idol they were waiting for—twenty-three-year-old Koda Mulvaney, heir to the billion-dollar Mulvaney real estate fortune—was already inside the studio, having entered through a secret underground entrance an hour earlier.

*   *   *

"Let's start with the question everyone wants the answer to," *BBC Sunday Morning Show* host Shelly Steele asked in a thick British accent. "What's it like to be the sexiest man alive?"

"Tiring," Koda Mulvaney said with a smile, followed by a slight laugh.

"Well, that would explain why you look a bit like something the cat dragged in."

"You've got a lot of great clubs in London," Koda said through a forced smile. "It would be impolite to not make an appearance."

"Interesting choice of words," Steele said flatly.

"Clubs?" Koda asked.

"No, I meant *appearance*," Steele said. "I hear that some celebrities—Paris Hilton and Kim Kardashian, for example—command fees of $10,000 and up to grace a club with their presence. Do you charge a fee for *your* appearances?"

Koda realized, a bit late, that this wasn't going to be a friendly interview. Steele had a reputation for being tough, and it was clear she'd taken the gloves off—and taken them off early at that.

"No, I do not charge a fee, Ms. Steele," Koda said through clenched teeth, knowing he should leave it there but somehow unable to stop himself: "My family has made $10 billion in the real estate business and charging a fee would be a bit crass, don't you think?"

"Let's talk about the profile *People* did on you," Steele said in an instant change of direction as she reached down and lifted a copy of the magazine from the glass table that separated them. "It says that your net worth is somewhere north of $2 billion, though you've never worked a day in your life. You usually sleep until mid-afternoon in a new city every day, and it goes on to say you broke off your engagement to Savannah socialite Mika Flagler two years ago, and it says you celebrated your twenty-third birthday partying with pals Kanye West and Channing Tatum at the Monaco Grand Prix and..."

"I know what the article says," Koda said, cutting her off. "Is there a question in my future? If so, I'd be thrilled if you got to it before I hit my twenty-fourth birthday."

"The question is: Why do you think women find you sexy? Is it because of your money, your looks, or charming personality?"

"Gee, I always thought it was the jet," Koda said to the laughter of the studio audience.

"Ah, yes. Your private love-nest in the sky," Steele said, pouncing on the opportunity.

Tiny when compared to Mark Cuban's Boeing 767-277, which had been fitted with custom seats large enough to accommodate the tallest Maverick players, Koda's smaller Bombardier BD-700 had become a significant part of his public persona. It could carry eight people at a cruising altitude of 51,000 feet for a distance of 6,500 nautical miles, a range that permitted the plane to fly nonstop from Tokyo to New York or Los Angeles to Moscow. It was outfitted with everything a jet-setting playboy really needed: a fully stocked bar and a king-sized bed.

Koda felt his cell phone vibrate in his pant pocket. Whoever it was would have to wait.

"You've been linked to Paris Hilton and too many Victoria's Secret models to name them all."

"Isn't that why they put out the catalogue?" Koda said. The audience laughed again.

"Interesting," Steele said, as if she were Koda's therapist. "Is that how you think of women? As products in a catalog you can simply shop for and then bed?"

Koda did not answer.

"My sources tell me you've nicknamed the plane Nisa," Steele continued. "One of your many conquests, I assume?"

Shit.

Koda had made a mistake, having opened the door to a topic he didn't want to discuss—especially on worldwide television and with a pounding hangover-headache no less.

"This Nisa must have been quite good in the sack to name your plane after her," Steele prompted.

"I never kiss and tell," Koda said, attempting to deflect the question as the cell phone began to vibrate once again.

"Come on, Koda, you can tell us," Steele said, egging him on. When he did not bite, she turned to the studio audience and said: "You want to know who Nisa is, don't you?"

A cheer went up.

There was nowhere to run.

Koda turned in his chair so he was squarely facing the show's host and leveled a glare at her before speaking. "Nisa is my mother's name—short for Manisamahpiya, her full Sioux Indian name."

"So, you named your love jet after the mother who abandoned you when you were six?" Steele asked to the gasps of the audience.

Koda had had enough and removed his microphone. "Is this how you treat all your guests?" Koda asked.

"No, just the cocky ones," Steele said. "Now, stop being a daft knob-head and finish the interview. Who knows, maybe I'll even let you show me that plane of yours when we're done."

"In your dreams," Koda said as he stood and dropped the mic on his chair as his cell phone began vibrating for the third time.

"You agreed to the full hour," Steele said.

"Sue me," Koda said over his shoulder, pulling his cell phone out of his pocket to see who wanted to reach him so badly. It wasn't one of his friends—no one he knew would call before two o'clock in the afternoon.

There were three text messages, short and to the point:

Watching the show, you look like shit.

Your trust fund is 100% depleted.

It's time to come home and go to work.

Koda didn't need to see who the messages were from. He already knew. Each had come from the same person in Orlando, Florida.

From his father.

ST. LOUIS, MISSOURI
AUGUST 5, 1904

O bedience Everhardt sat in front of the bedroom mirror, working her long gray hair into a braided pony tail that, when she was finished, hung down her back almost to her knees. She then stood and went to the closet to choose exactly the right dress. "What about the blue one?" she asked aloud and waited for her daughter to answer. Yes, the blue dress was the perfect choice.

It had worked every time before, hadn't it?

Obedience buttoned the front of the pale blue garment and placed her long, braided ponytail over her shoulder. How long has it been since I cut it last? Long ago, she thought. So long, in fact, that she could not remember exactly when it had been.

Perhaps it was the year she and Titus had moved here to St. Louis, during the early years of the war, before he was called to serve. "So unfair," she said aloud to her daughter. Titus had moved the three of them to Missouri specifically because it was a neutral state that wanted no part in the conflict between the North and the South. And then, unexpectedly, things changed and Titus was called to serve anyway.

"So very unfair," Obedience said again.

No, it must have been later, Obedience realized as she slipped on a pair of brown knee-high boots and pulled tightly on the laces. Lucinda was already in school, so it had to have been sometime after 1864.

Her thought was interrupted by the sounds of a girl's screams from the floor below. Screams that could barely be heard from inside the house and could not be heard whatsoever from the street. No one was ever invited into their home.

Not ever.

Just herself and Lucinda, they were the only ones allowed— oh, and Titus, of course, whenever he returned from the war. He'd written and said he was on his way. The South had surrendered. He would be coming on a ship with other prisoners of war who'd also been released. He would be home any day.

Obedience stood and examined herself in the mirror, from head to toe.

The outfit said simple...

The outfit said safe...

The outfit said she was a mature woman who wouldn't hurt a fly, that she could be trusted... that there was no reason to be afraid. It was perfect.

Obedience walked into the main sitting room and grabbed her shawl, the screams from the cellar a bit louder now, in part because this was the closest point in the house to where the girl was tied in her chair, but also because she was a smart girl.

The girl's time was up.

"It's almost time for your birthday, isn't it, Lucinda?" Obedience asked aloud, again waiting for an answer from someone only she could hear. "That's right," she said, a smile forming on her face: "time for your birthday party."

For the final touch, Obedience pinned the button she'd been given by the fair organizers to the front of her dress. "Ask Me, I Live Here," the button declared in bold red letters.

Yes, you look safe and helpful, Obedience thought.

Now, where exactly should she go to find her new Lucinda? The fairgrounds were enormous, with so many options. But Obedience knew there was really only one perfect place.

The Ferris wheel.

Children just loved the Ferris wheel.

SAVANNAH, GEORGIA
JUNE 2, 1979

The last person Quinn Cole expected to see standing at his door was his high school friend, Wyatt Scrogger.

"How's it hanging, dropout?" Scrogger asked as Quinn opened the door. "What's it been, a year?"

Two, Quinn thought, but who's counting. "Nice you could finally stop by," Quinn said.

Quinn and Wyatt had been best friends since the fifth grade, when Quinn was about to get his ass kicked by four schoolyard bullies. Wyatt had stepped from the group of onlookers: "Hey, did you guys hear that new Helen Keller joke? Don't worry, neither did she."

The bullies stared at Wyatt.

Wyatt stayed with it. "So, why can't Helen Keller drive? Because she's a woman, get it?"

He got a snicker from one of the four.

"How do you get Helen Keller to keep a secret? Break her fingers."

All four began to laugh, so Scrogger went in for the knockout: "How did Helen Keller's parents punish her for swearing? They washed her hands with soap. How did Helen Keller burn her face? She tried to answer the iron."

As far as Quinn was concerned, the jokes weren't funny but they had the intended effect on the bullies. The guys laughed, then seemed to forget what they were after, somehow disarmed by Wyatt's sense of humor.

Quinn had come to learn that Wyatt Scrogger could be a complete ass sometimes, but he had saved his bacon that day and they'd been close ever since. When Quinn dropped out of college, they'd sort of lost touch with each other.

Scrogger slid past Quinn and went straight to the kitchen, opened the refrigerator door and started searching around. "Milk, orange juice, Fresca," Scrogger said. "No beer?"

Quinn did not answer. When Wyatt looked up, Quinn held up a single index finger and pointed at the ceiling.

"Oh," Scrogger said, lowering his voice. "Your mom's on the sauce again, huh?"

"Never really stopped," Quinn said. "Days go by she doesn't even bother to get dressed."

"What about your dad?" Scrogger asked.

Quinn shook his head. Scrogger had known things were bad at home for Quinn, which was why he'd made the decision to drop out of college the middle of his freshman year, but he had no idea that Quinn had literally become the man of the family.

"I had no idea" was the only thing Scrogger could think to say.

"How could you possibly," Quinn said.

"Listen," Scrogger said, "I've got a few bucks from some gigs I've been doing. How about you and I go get a pizza and a pitcher or two, catch up on things?"

"Bad timing," Quinn said. "Juniper's heading off to the prom in a bit—"

"Juniper's here?" Scrogger asked. "Cool, I want to see her."

"She's in the shower and..."

"Who is that?" a voice called out from the second floor of the house.

"Sounds like she's out," Scrogger said.

Scrogger left the kitchen and headed back toward the front door, near the base of the stairs, Quinn trailing behind. "Is that you, carrot top?" Scrogger yelled. "Get your scrawny little freckled-butt down here. I've got some new jokes I want to try..."

Wyatt Scrogger stopped mid-sentence, his mouth literally hanging open.

Quinn caught up to Scrogger and the two of them watched as Juniper made her way slowly down the stairs toward them, being careful not to trip on her powder-blue prom dress.

"Wow, now that's a dress," Scrogger said.

"Be careful, that's my sister," Quinn said.

Juniper reached the bottom of the stairs and threw herself into Wyatt Scrogger's arms and hugged him: "I missed you, Scroggs!"

"Did you hear me mention that's my sister?" Quinn asked.

"Step back, let me take a look at you," Scrogger said as he released her and looked her over. "Same red hair, same freckles. Holy crap, Juniper, you grew boobs!" Scrogger turned to Quinn: "You're going along with her tonight as a chaperone, right?"

"Jesus," Quinn said under his breath, though he knew it was useless. And though he knew his friend was simply joking around—as he always did—Quinn found himself feeling uncomfortable. "She's a grown woman, Scroggs, Juniper can take care of herself," Quinn said, hoping it was true.

"How's college?" Juniper asked. "Great, I'll bet."

"Yeah, I'm majoring in girls and minoring in pick-up lines," Scrogger said, "doing some small clubs at night."

"Tell me some jokes," Juniper said. She loved jokes and could always count on Scrogger for an endless stream of them.

Scrogger said, "Okay, Carrot Top, you play the gorgeous girl sitting at the bar and I'll be the obnoxious guy who's trying to pick you up."

"Wait until I get in character," Juniper said, lifting a pretend drink in her hand and then looking away as if totally disinterested. "Okay, go ahead and pick me up."

Scrogger reached out, tapped Juniper on the shoulder. "Excuse me, miss? I was wondering if I could take your picture because I'd like to show Santa exactly what I want for Christmas."

Juniper fought off the urge to smile. "Please, sir, may I have another?" she said.

"Your father must have been a baker, because you've got great buns," Scrogger said.

"That's pretty good," Juniper said, "It could actually work."

"Did you hear me earlier when I mentioned she's my sister?" Quinn interjected.

"Quinn, we're just playing," Juniper said. "More, please."

"If I could rearrange the alphabet, do you think U and I could be together?" Scrogger said and Juniper burst out laughing.

"If you were a booger, I'd pick you first," Scrogger said, then:

"That must be a space suit you're wearing because your body is out of this world..."

"Excuse me, I'm new in town and I was hoping you could give me directions to your place..."

"It's a good thing I brought my library card with me tonight because I'm totally checking you out..."

"Okay, stop, you win," Juniper said. "I'll go out with you."

"Over my dead body," Quinn said a bit too seriously.

"Accept it, man, your sister is the mayor of Woodville," Scrogger said. Then to Juniper: "Juniper, you're still playing the piano, right?"

Juniper looked away and said nothing.

"She's taking a break," Quinn said. "As soon as she turns 18—"

"In less than a year," Juniper said.

"Then she can legally sign documents and be in control of her own accounts."

"I don't get it," Scrogger said. "What?"

"Our dad drained all of Juniper's accounts—every penny she'd made in appearance and recording fees from the age of five to the age of sixteen—then ran off with some bimbo he'd met on a business trip to California."

"He'll come back," Juniper said.

"Dad is gone, Juniper. He is *never* coming back. I won't let him."

Juniper turned her back on Quinn, leaned toward Wyatt and kissed him on the cheek. "Nice seeing you, Scroggs. We missed you." Then Juniper hiked up her dress and started up the stairs: "If you gentlemen will excuse me, I have a date with a curling iron."

"Sorry things have been so rough for you, man," Scrogger said after Juniper was gone. "You sure you don't want to head out for a few beers?"

"No, but thanks," Quinn said. "Juniper's date is going to be here in a half hour or so, and I've got to be here to give him the talk."

Scrogger shot Quinn a look. "The talk?"

"Yeah, you know. The talk fathers give to their daughter's boyfriends, the one where I threaten to kill the poor son of a bitch if he so much as looks at her wrong."

"You're a good brother, Quinn."

FROM THE JOURNAL OF ONYX WEBB

My name is Onyx Webb, and I have a story to tell, a number of them actually. But for now, I intend to share just one... Mine.

Not all of it, mind you, but enough to understand the basics of my life: Where I was born, how I ended up marrying the wrong man, and why he wanted me dead. How I came to live in the old lighthouse on Crimson Cove, and—of course—how I ended up being a ghost.

The event that changed my life, or, more accurately, ended it, occurred 75 years ago as of this writing. As far as the universe is concerned, three-quarters of a century is a very brief time.

I should know.

Should I choose, I can literally exist forever.

Please notice that I didn't say "live" forever. Living people eat food and drink wine. The living can experience fun and joy and happiness. The living can cry real tears and have human hearts that beat.

And they feel love.

For a ghost, none of this is possible. To make my existence even worse, there is something I must do... something ugly, something inherently evil.

To maintain my existence in the living plane, I must...

Kill.

I know what you are wondering: if what I must do is so intolerable, why continue? There are two reasons:

First, my existence—as empty and vapid as it may seem—is the closest thing to life I have, and life is a very hard thing to let go of—even in death.

And then there is the other reason, the oldest reason there is. I have met a man. A man who may finally be "the one," a man who may love me the way a woman should be loved. He is a man who may finally bring me the joy and happiness I have thirsted for.

And he knows the truth. He knows that I am not the living woman I had portrayed myself to be.

And yet, even with the knowledge, he still professes his love.

He says I am everything he's ever wanted, and that I make him feel whole...

that he can't live without me.

And to prove it, he did something I am forbidden to do for myself. He gathered my bones, long scattered beneath the tall pines these many years, and buried my body. At least, the little that remained.

How's that for a demonstration of love?

The question now is: Will my cold hands and dead heart be enough for him?

Equally as important, will it be enough for me?

ORLANDO, FLORIDA
JANUARY 11, 2010

Koda Mulvaney gazed out the jet's window and could see Orlando International Airport off in the distance, the runways looking like Band-Aids, applied haphazardly in a crisscross pattern, to the wounded earth below.

Several miles beyond was Orlando Executive Airport, where Mulvaney Properties International—MPI, for short—maintained a private hangar that housed three additional planes: his father's Bombardier Global XRS, a Gulfstream V used as a loaner to lure corporate clients, and an old 14-cylinder, 8-passenger Boeing Vultee, which belonged to a friend of his grandfather's whom he'd never met. To the best of Koda's knowledge, the Vultee hadn't been in the air in over 40 years.

"I still don't understand why you hate your old man so much," Dane Luckner said, sitting in his usual seat across from Koda.

Dane was not only Koda Mulvaney's best friend, he was his only friend. His only true friend, at least.

Like most super-wealthy people, Koda was surrounded by hordes of acquaintances—people who claimed they were friends—as long as the party invitations and free drinks kept coming.

But Dane Luckner was different. Dane could not have cared less. Yes, the last two years jet-setting around the world had been amazing, but he didn't hang with Koda because Koda paid the tab.

The pair had bonded during a lacrosse match their sophomore year at Syracuse when a Dartmouth player slashed Koda across the face with his stick. Though he'd never been much of a fighter, the sight of blood gushing from the two-inch gash set Dane off. It took three players and two referees to pull him off.

Koda's father, Bruce, had taken an instant liking to Dane, having witnessed the entire event from the stands. He'd flown in for the weekend, along with Koda's grandfather, Declan Mulvaney—who'd started the family business fifty years earlier—and Bruce's limo driver and bodyguard, Tank.

"Who is that guy?" Declan had asked.

"His name is Dane," Bruce said. "Dane Luckner."

"Whoever it is, he just became Koda's new BFF," Tank said.

"BF what?" Declan Mulvaney asked. Declan had just celebrated his eighty-third birthday and refused to own a cell phone.

"It's an abbreviation, Dad," Bruce said. "It means best friends forever."

Declan shook his head. "Why does everything have to be abbreviated?"

"It's easier when you're texting," Tank said.

Declan watched as Dane continued wailing on the poor Dartmouth player who's only defense was to curl up in a ball like a frightened possum. "This Luckner kid, I like him. He's got spunk."

It had been four years since that day, and Koda and Dane had been as inseparable as Siamese twins.

"I like your dad," Dane said.

"That's because you haven't met him," Koda said.

"Not true. I met him at Syracuse," Dane said, pointing at the scar: "The day you got that."

Koda reached up and ran his fingers across the scar. "Well, he was on his best behavior because my grandfather was there."

*   *   *

The jet's wheels grabbed the runway and rolled to a stop, approximately one-hundred feet from the MPI corporate hangar. Bruce Mulvaney, dressed in a $10,000 charcoal gray Ozwald Boateng suit, leaned against the limousine, waiting.

"Hello, Dane," Bruce Mulvaney said as the two 23-year-olds made their way toward the black stretch limo parked near the large hangar doors.

"Hey, Mr. Mulvaney," Dane said. Dane reached out and shook Bruce's hand.

The driver's door opened and a heavy-set Samoan clad in a black Armani suit stepped out. "Hey, Dane. Hey, Koda," Tank called out. "I tried to tell your dad this was a bad idea, meeting here in the dark like this, but you know your dad."

Bruce Mulvaney turned, shot Tank a look.

"Don't go giving me the evil eye, Boss," Tank said. "You know this could have waited until tomorrow morning."

"No, it couldn't," Bruce said. "My son doesn't know what morning is, but he's going to learn, starting now."

Koda stopped about five feet from his father, but—unlike Dane—he did not reach out to shake his father's hand.

"You two have a nice vacation?" Bruce asked.

"It was great, thanks." Dane said.

"Don't thank me, Dane," Bruce said. "Thank Koda. Every dime of your escapades came from his account, not mine."

"Too short if you ask me," Koda said.

"Long, short, whatever," Bruce said. "The important thing is that it's over."

"Why did you make us come back?" Koda asked. "And what did you mean about my trust fund being empty? That's not possible."

"Exactly," Bruce said. "How could anyone possibly run through $20 million in nineteen months?"

Dane turned to Koda, silently mouthed: "Twenty million?"

Koda shrugged.

"It seemed impossible," Bruce Mulvaney continued. "So I had the office pull the billing files on the jet and asked American Express to forward copies of the statements for your Black Card for the last nineteen months."

Bruce held out his hand, palm up. Tank stepped forward and placed a thick manila file folder in Bruce's hand then took a step back.

"You know what it cost to fly a BD-700?"

Koda stayed silent.

"I didn't think so," Bruce said. "$5,192 per hour, that's how much. You got any idea how many hours you had the plane in the air?"

Koda stayed silent.

"2,280 hours. At $5,192 per hour, that comes to $11,800,000. Add another $2.5 million for landing fees, towing, hangar rental—we're talking $14.3 million, Koda, just for the plane."

Koda stayed silent.

"But let's not forget the pilots who fly the plane," Bruce continued. "Add $250,000 per year for the pilot's salary, and another $150,000 for the co-pilot—plus two extremely generous benefit packages—and we've got another $600,000."

Koda stayed silent.

"That's a lot of money, Koda, even to us," Bruce said. "And I haven't even gotten to the stupid stuff yet."

Bruce pulled out a second sheet of paper, waved it in the air. "According to American Express, you put the pilots up at the Four Seasons—in separate rooms, no less—at $400 per night, per room. Add room service and alcohol and in-room movies and tips, we're talking another $750,000. Am I getting your attention?"

Koda stayed silent.

Bruce rattled on: "Food, $322,000; alcohol, $730,000; tips, $280,000. But the next one is the one that really floored me,"

Bruce snapped. "Do you have any idea how many bottles of Cristal the two of you ran through?"

"You can't blame me for any of that, sir," Dane interjected. "I don't drink champagne."

"Shut up, Dane," Bruce said. "The answer is 3,422 bottles at $300 each. That's over $1 million on champagne ... for people you probably don't even know and who probably don't even like you."

Koda stayed silent.

"Jeez," Dane said under his breath to Koda. "I knew we were having a good time, but I had no idea it was that good."

Bruce continued. "Hotel, $1.2 million—again, with each of you getting your own room."

"I need my privacy," Koda said, speaking at last: "After all, I am the sexiest man alive."

"I wouldn't push it, Koda," Tank said loudly. "I've been with your dad all day, and he is really pissed. Plus, some of that shit? It's pretty excessive, even by Mulvaney standards."

"That comes to $20.5 million, Koda. And do you want to hear the final kicker? You forgot to settle your account when you left the Intercontinental Hotel in Amsterdam. It went to collections, so technically you are now formally $500,000 in debt and have ruined your credit."

"You could have taken care of that if you'd wanted to," Koda said.

"True," Bruce said, "but it wasn't my bill, it was yours. And *your* bills are *your* responsibility. Jesus, you act like you're entitled to everything. You're like a welfare recipient, but with a much bigger check."

"So what's your point?" Koda asked.

"The point is, you start work tomorrow morning, annual salary of $71,500, the same entry-level pay we offer to all recruits out of college," Bruce said. "I expect you to be in the office promptly at 8:30 a.m. You can stay in the corporate suite across the street from the office. The refrigerator is stocked with food. When you run out, you can buy more with money you earn like the rest of the world. You will also represent the company at the Restoring Savannah Foundation dinner at the end of the month at the Forsyth Park Hotel. Mika Flagler will be co-hosting the event with you, and she will be your date for the night. Am I understood?" Bruce asked.

Koda released an audible groan. "I feel like I just got trapped in a nightmare version of Arthur."

"Are we clear?" Bruce asked again.

"This is the part where you say yes, Koda, and we all go home," Tank said.

"Yeah, we're clear," Koda said.

"I'm flying to Charleston. Tank's got the keys to the apartment and will take you downtown," Bruce said. "Get a good night's sleep, you look like hell. Wear a coat and tie, and make sure you're clean-shaven—none of this three-day-stubble-shit."

Bruce leaned forward, put his arms around Koda and hugged him. "I love you, even if you don't believe it. I'll see you in the morning."

Koda did not hug him back.

ST. LOUIS, MISSOURI
AUGUST 6, 1904

The 1904 World's Fair in St. Louis, Missouri—created to celebrate the hundredth anniversary of the Louisiana Purchase—promised to be the most important gathering of notable scientists, artists, inventors, celebrities, business titans, and political leaders in the history of man.

And it did not disappoint.

Thomas Edison was there, as was President Theodore Roosevelt, ragtime musician Scott Joplin, and distiller Jack Daniel, who entered his Tennessee elixir into the World's Fair whiskey competition.

John Philip Sousa performed the opening march, T.S. Elliott did a poetry reading, and Helen Keller—with the aid of an assistant—delivered a presentation that brought people to tears.

The fair also introduced the world to the ice cream cone, peanut butter, iced tea, cotton candy and an odd-tasting drink called Dr. Pepper.

That morning, just before they arrived at St. Louis Station, Catfish surprised Onyx with the camera she'd begged him for— a Kodak Brownie that had commanded the princely sum of $4.

Within minutes of entering the gate, Onyx was loading film and taking pictures, Catfish encouraging her at every turn. "You snap everything you wish, Jitterbug," the big man said. "In the end, all any of us gonna have will be memories, so make 'em good as you can." The only thing Catfish would not allow her to photograph was Geronimo. It broke his heart to see the great Apache warrior put on display for two-cents a picture, bow and arrow in his frail hands like movie props. He simply would not permit it.

"I wish your mama and I had one of these when we went to the fair," Catfish said.

"You went to a fair with Mama?" Onyx asked.

"Chicago, 'fore you were born," Catfish said. "Your mama never cared much for having her picture taken, so I never saw a need to own one, till now."

Onyx possessed a single out-of-focus black & white of her mother, taken years before she'd been born. It remained, to this day, her most important possession.

Catfish had given Onyx a brochure on the various exhibits weeks earlier, instructing her to make a list of the ten things she wanted to do most. The size and scope of the fairgrounds—1,500 buildings connected by seventy-five miles of roads and walkways over 1,250 acres—made it impossible to take more than a glance at everything, even if staying a week.

"What are the first things you want to do, Jitterbug?" Catfish asked.

"Ten things, right?" Onyx said.

"We might get to mor'n ten," Catfish said, "but how 'bout we start with that. Well?"

Onyx had worked diligently assembling her list. But where should they go first? That was easy. "The Ferris Wheel!" Onyx yelled without hesitation. And after an hour in line, Catfish and Onyx were looking down on the thousands of fairgoers 300 feet below. Less than a year earlier, the Wright Brothers had flown like birds in the sky, and now Onyx had, too. She was on the ride for less than 20 minutes, but it would be the best 20 minutes of her life.

"You and I get separated, we both come here to the Ferris Wheel, Onyx," Catfish told her when they'd gotten off.

Onyx nodded, but her mind was still soaring.

* * *

It was just after lunch when Catfish saw the sign: "Hunting Competition, 2 p.m., First Prize a 6-inch Landers Frary & Clark Hunting Knife!" Catfish was a man who loved a challenge. He also needed a new knife.

When it was time for the competition to start, Catfish knelt down and made eye contact with his daughter. "Stay here, child, don't you be runnin' off on me." Unfortunately, there were two things Catfish hadn't taken into consideration. The first was how long the competition would take, and the second was the impatience of a six year old. No matter how many times he reminded himself to glance over and check on her, the competition demanded his full attention.

Catfish stood on the small make-shift platform, first-place prize in hand as a photographer from the *St. Louis Post-Dispatch* set up his camera. He peered in the direction where he'd left his daughter but couldn't see her. He leaned to his left, then his right. No, Onyx.

"Everyone smile!" said the photographer, looking through the camera lens to discover the top step of the award stand was now empty.

*   *   *

Catfish sprinted into the crowd, frantically searching for any sign of Onyx but she was nowhere to be seen. "Onyx!" he yelled. "Anyone seen a young girl, 'bout this tall," he said, panic starting to rise in his throat. "She be holdin' a camera?"

No one responded. No one had seen her. Catfish cupped his hands around his mouth. "Onyx!" he screamed, spinning in circles, looking in every direction.

Catfish kept spinning, calling her name, frantically searching the fairgrounds and people's faces, and then he saw it...

The Ferris wheel.

Catfish sprinted toward the enormous revolving structure as fast as his legs would carry him—bumping into fairgoers, knocking one man to the ground. He stopped near the ticket booth, gasping for air, eyes searching once again in every direction.

And then he spotted her, walking about thirty yards away in the opposite direction, holding a woman's hand.

"Onyx!" Catfish screamed.

The young girl turned...

It was her.

She waved at him. Thank God, Catfish thought.

Catfish started toward her, relief washing over him like a cleansing rain, but then something unexpected happened.

The woman turned, made direct eye contact with him, grabbed Onyx by the wrist, and started to run.

*　　*　　*

"Tell me again," said Detective Stormy Boyd, sitting in a chair and scribbling in a notepad. "She called her what...?"

"She had my Onyx, and she was running away," Catfish said as an emergency room doctor tugged on the needle, making sure the stitch was tight. With a jagged wound of this nature—a full six inches in length, running down the left side of his face from forehead to jawline, the most skillful stitching in the world wouldn't reduce the size of the scar or return sight to his eye. "She kept calling my daughter Lucinda, over and over, ranting like a screech owl. But I told you this already, detective."

Catfish was frustrated, having explained the entire series of events repeatedly. "I chased the gray-haired woman, she had Onyx. They went into the Libby Glass Company exhibit, and I kept screaming for the woman to stop. Then I turned a corner without knowing there was a ceiling-to-floor plate glass window as part of a display."

Boyd nodded, scribbled on his notepad. "And that's when the woman got away, and you say she had gray hair?"

Catfish winced as the doctor pulled on the needle for the forty-third time, still a few stitches away from completion. "Yes, the woman with the long gray hair," Catfish repeated, "ran all the way down to her buttocks and..."

Suddenly Catfish remembered a small detail he'd forgotten until that moment. "There is something, detective. The woman was wearing a button of some kind."

Stormy Boyd looked up from his notepad. "A white button? Do you remember what it said?"

"No, but I think it had red letters," Catfish said.

"Could it have been, *'Ask Me, I Live Here'?*" Boyd prompted.

"Yes! That is exactly what it said. What does it mean?"

"It means she's a volunteer," Boyd said.

"So, her name must be on a list of some sort," Catfish said.

"Perhaps," Boyd said cautiously, closing his notebook. "Mr. Webb, you seem to me like a man who wants to know exactly how it is, so may I speak frankly?"

"That's all I ask, detective," Catfish said.

"There's a chance I know what happened to your daughter, Mr. Webb, and it's not good."

Catfish felt like he'd just had the air knocked out of him. "I don't understand..."

"Your daughter is not the first girl who's been taken," Boyd said, forging on. "By my count, I believe she's the seventh."

"The other six..." Catfish started, his words trailing off.

"They were found, eventually," Boyd said.

Bombs were exploding inside the Cajun's head. "Found? Found how?" Catfish asked. "How were they found?"

"Dead, Mr. Webb, they were all found dead," Boyd said.

"But you goin' to look for her? Correct? The police gonna put men out on the street and..."

"The biggest event in the history of the world is happening right here, right now. There are no men to put on the street, Mr. Webb, and I can't justify pulling someone off another detail when the chances of finding your little girl..."

"Onyx," Catfish interrupted, "my daughter's name is Onyx. All this time we been talkin' you haven't said her name aloud, not one time. You been talkin' 'bout her like she nothing more than a number in some report you can just file away. Well, you can't, I won't allow it. Say her name, detective."

"Mr. Webb, I understand..."

"Say her name, detective, speak it out loud right now."

"Onyx," Boyd said. "Your daughter's name is Onyx."

"You know the Lord's Prayer, detective?" Catfish asked.

"Yes, I do. And if it would be of comfort I'd be glad to recite it with you," Boyd said, reaching out to take Catfish's hand.

"I didn't ask for my sake, detective," Catfish said, "I asked for yours."

SAVANNAH, GEORGIA
JUNE 2, 1979

espite Quinn's rules, admonitions and a few direct threats to Juniper's prom date, the boy made his first move within minutes of climbing in the back of the stretch limousine. The constant barrage of lured comments, unwanted physical advances—and when that didn't work, outright begging—continued all night.

"What is it about guys?" Juniper asked a friend after seeking refuge in the safety of the women's restroom. Watching her father make passes at waitresses and flight attendants during the seven years he paraded her around the country had caused her to question the motives of all men at an early age. After all, if her dad—whom she totally adored—was a total sleaze-ball, what were the chances she'd end up with a great man someday?

"It's the prom, Juniper," her friend said as she applied another layer of red lipstick to her already-red lips. "I mean, you've gotta give it up sometime, right? It might as well be in a cool hotel."

That was helpful.

Juniper glanced at the clock, saw it was eleven o'clock, and made the decision to spend the next hour exploring the hotel and surrounding grounds instead of returning to the ballroom.

After gazing at the hotel's art collection, Juniper wandered around the pool area and sculpture gardens, ending up in the oldest part of the building where she saw a black Blasius & Sons grand piano.

How long had it been since she'd even placed her fingers on the keyboard? Six months? A year? She wasn't even sure if she could play anymore, at least not to the standards to which the concert community would expect from a world-class pianist.

She was tempted to take a seat and play.

But didn't.

At 11:45 p.m., Juniper walked through the hotel's large front doors and out to the street. Across Drayton Street, on the northern side of Forsyth Park, she could see a brightly lit fountain. Realizing she had fifteen minutes before the limousine would be coming to pick them up, Juniper stepped off the curb and crossed the street.

As she walked down the path toward the fountain, Juniper remembered performing there once, when she was ten or eleven.

She wondered if it was the same one they turned green on St. Patrick's Day. It looked like the one, she thought as she stood at the wrought-iron fence that surrounded the gleaming fountain.

And that's when the inspiration hit her.

Should I? Heck, why not? It would at least make prom night memorable for a good reason. Besides, what's the worst that could happen? They'd come and arrest her? She could see the headline: *Child Piano Prodigy Arrested Barefoot in Park Fountain.*

Juniper gathered her dress up to her hips and swung her left leg over the metal railing, then her right leg, and dropped to the ground. As someone who prided herself on following the rules, Juniper felt a certain degree of excitement knowing she was officially trespassing.

Juniper hiked up the bottom of her prom dress so as not to ruin the delicate chiffon material by getting it wet—her tan legs exposed beneath her—and jumped into the gleaming white fountain.

Looking down, Juniper could see the gold ankle-bracelet—sparkling and shimmering in the water—a gift from Quinn for her sixteenth birthday.

And then she heard a horn blare in the distance.

Juniper gazed across the park toward the hotel and could see the long line of limousines pulling out, one after the other.

It was midnight.

Juniper climbed from the fountain as fast as she could, scaled the small metal barricade and began *fast-waddling* toward the hotel, which was all she could manage in her tight-fitting gown.

She reached Drayton Street just as the last of the limousines pulled from the hotel driveway and disappeared into the darkness.

ORLANDO, FLORIDA
JANUARY 12, 2010

Koda had the dream again. It was the same dream he'd had his entire life.

In the dream, Koda is six years old, wandering through the basement of his house, which was a palatial mansion on the outskirts of Charleston, South Carolina—built on the site of the historic Stono Slave Rebellion. It was the house where Bruce Mulvaney had grown up, and then Koda as well.

The dream began with Koda wandering aimlessly from room to room, until—inevitably—he would hear a woman screaming. He would follow the sound of the screams, getting louder and louder, but every time he thought he'd found the source, they would simply fade away.

Then the screams would begin again.

But it wasn't simply the woman's screams that terrified him—it was the knowledge that the woman who was screaming was his mother.

"Where are you?" Koda calls out, running frantically from room to room until he could make out her words.

"Help me... help me... please... please... please..."

Suddenly he knows where the screams are coming from— they're coming from the other side of the wall.

He looks for something to use to break through the wall, but there is nothing, so he begins clawing at the bricks with his fingers until they are raw and bleeding.

Then the screams stop.

Koda curls into a ball on the floor and begins to sob.

He knows he has failed her.

He knows his father has failed her.

And he knows he will never see her again.

* * *

When Koda woke from the dream—bathed in sweat, his face wet with tears—it took a full minute to get his bearings as to where he was.

He was in the master bedroom in MPI's penthouse apartment on the thirty-first floor of the 55 West building in downtown Orlando. Because the building sat directly across the street from the iconic beige-and-green SunTrust building where Mulvaney Properties offices occupied the twenty-sixth and twenty-seventh floors, Koda could look out the window and actually see into his father's office.

The clock read 5:30 p.m. and things came back to him.

The day—his first day at work—had not started well.

Though Bruce had warned him to be on time, Koda overslept and walked into the office at 9:10 a.m.

"Even after I warned you to be on time, you have the audacity to drag your sorry ass in here forty minutes late?" Bruce said, loudly enough for all to hear. "Go home and pull yourself together, and be here on time tomorrow. And if you ever come in here stinking of alcohol again, I swear I'll fire your ass and you can go to work flipping burgers at McDonalds."

Koda rolled from the bed, pulled on a pair of gym shorts and made his way into the living room where he found Dane sitting on the sofa deeply involved in a game of *Resident Evil V*.

"Watch out for the spike ceiling," Koda said.

Dane stopped playing and looked up, shocked to see Koda standing there. "What are you doing here? I thought you were at work?"

"Long story," Koda said. "Get dressed, I'm hungry."

"Can you afford it?" Dane asked.

The question hit him hard. This was the first time in his life Koda had to even think about what things cost, and if he could afford it. Maybe his father was right—maybe he was a welfare baby.

He walked to the kitchen counter, opened his wallet. He had two credit cards, which he wasn't entirely sure were still active, and $346 in cash. Was that enough to buy dinner with? He didn't know. He hadn't looked at the price column on a menu in his life.

"Yeah, I got a few bucks," he said. "Let's go."

*　　*　　*

When Koda and Dane walked through the front doors of the 55 West building onto Church Street, the first thing they noticed was what they *didn't* see: throngs of screaming girls waving signs reading *"Marry Me, Koda."* No one knew Koda was in Orlando.

And it was nice.

"There," Koda said.

The place was called *DJ's Chophouse.* With twenty-five-foot-high ceilings and amazing architecture, the restaurant occupied the bottom floor of an old five-and-dime. Upscale in every way, *DJ's* served prime dry-aged steaks and strong drinks, catering specifically to Orlando's movers and shakers who flooded into the city during the day.

It was perfect.

Koda and Dane took seats at the bar and an attractive brunette approached. "Hi, I'm Robyn. So, what can I get for the sexiest guy I've ever seen?" the bartender asked.

"Tito's on the rocks," Koda said.

"No, I meant him," Robyn said pointing to Dane. "You? You look like hell."

"I get that a lot lately," Koda said, slightly annoyed.

"I'll have an Amstel Light," Dane said.

"She's funny," Dane said as she walked away.

"She likes you," Koda said. "And she's got a great ass."

"She was just being friendly," Dane said.

Koda shrugged. "Maybe, but might be worth a shot."

When the drinks arrived, Robyn watched as Koda tipped his head back and downed his vodka then ordered another.

Robyn turned to Dane. "Is your friend intelligent?"

"Smart?" Dane asked. "That's a loaded question. But seeing that Koda is sitting right here, I'm going with yes."

"Why do you ask?" Koda said.

"Because it looks like you're in the fast lane to getting seriously hammered," Robyn said. "Don't get me wrong—I personally don't care if you drink yourself into oblivion—but as a professional bartender I'm required to cut you off if I determine you've had too much, and differentiating between being very drunk and the simply stupid is a tough task."

After a few seconds of silence, Koda managed a response. "Do you know who I am?"

"Of course," Robyn said. "Koda Mulvaney, son of Bruce Mulvaney and grandson of Declan Mulvaney, heir to the Mulvaney fortune and recently crowned sexiest man alive."

"You got all that from *People*?" Koda snorted.

"No, I got all that from your father," Robyn said. "Your dad comes in here two times a week, puts back a few double martinis, and then when he's good and relaxed he pulls out his wallet and shows your picture to anyone who will look. It must be wonderful having a dad who loves you so much."

ST. LOUIS, MISSOURI
AUGUST 7, 1904

When Catfish Webb finally left the emergency room at the fairgrounds, he was in shock, pain, and a state of physical exhaustion. The last thing he could afford was to lose time sleeping, but he had no other choice.

After a fitful nights' sleep and still in excruciating pain, Catfish found the St. Louis public library. He read the various newspaper accounts regarding "The St. Louis Child Snatcher" and the six victims whose bodies had been discovered over the years. The last girl to be taken—Katherine Keane—had gone missing six years earlier and had yet to surface.

No one, including the police, had come up with a viable theory for the abductions, but the pattern was clear: a young girl would go missing, and two or three days later the previous girl's body would be found. It was always a bizarre scene, according to the reports.

Each with a scar running through both the top and bottom lip, where several teeth had either been knocked out or pulled.

Each girl so pasty-white she looked as if she had not seen sunlight in years.

Each in a yellow, hand-embroidered dress, with a pair of white, patent-leather shoes set on the ground next to the body as they were several sizes too small to fit.

Despondent but with no options left, Catfish returned to the fairgrounds. He sat on a bench close to where he and Onyx had first entered the previous day.

He looked at his watch and realized that he'd lost Onyx within five hours of walking through the fair's front gates. Small tears formed in the corners of his eyes at first, turning into deep uncontrollable sobs.

Then a miracle happened.

Catfish was not a religious man, and not one to believe in miracles, but what happened next truly was.

A young boy walked by holding a Kodak Brownie camera and Catfish heard him ask, "Daddy, can I take a picture of the Indian?"

Geronimo.

Onyx had gone to take a picture of Geronimo.

Catfish closed his eyes and replayed the events of the previous afternoon. The woman holding Onyx by her left hand, *which was empty*—and how Onyx had turned and waved with her other hand.

It had been empty, as well.

Catfish jumped to his feet and began to run.

*   *   *

Stormy Boyd could not get Catfish Webb out of his head. Boyd wasn't fearful over what the man might do to him should the worst occur. He feared the regret of knowing he hadn't done everything within his power to help.

The only lead of value was the white button Webb said he'd seen pinned to the woman's dress. If she *was* an official volunteer at the fair, not someone who had simply found the button or stolen it, then her name would indeed be on a list. The question was: how big a list?

It took less than an hour for Stormy to use his position to secure the list, which was as sizeable as he had feared: 586 people, all from the St. Louis area, who'd replied to newspaper advertisements offering free passage into the fairgrounds in exchange for volunteering.

When he was young, Stormy used to sit on the porch of the family cabin in the Ozark Mountains and watch his father literally "whittle away" the day. Over time, it had become a game between the two of them. His father would grab a piece of oak or pine and pull out his knife.

"What do you think is inside this one, son?" Stormy's father would ask.

"I don't know, Daddy, a duck maybe?" Stormy would reply, playing along, choosing a different animal each time.

"A duck, huh?" his father would say with a sly smile. "Well, what do you say we find out?"

Then Stormy would sit there for the next hour and watch as—bit by bit, cut by cut, chip by chip—the knife would whittle away whatever wasn't inside, eventually exposing what was.

The lesson had served him well as a detective, because whittling was what detective Stormy Boyd excelled at most.

He started with what he knew. They were looking for a woman. Based on her gray hair, and the date the first girl disappeared, she was at least fifty. And the woman had, or once had, a daughter named Lucinda.

Boyd whittled away every man on the list, reducing it from 568 names to 391.

By a stroke of good fortune, the organizers had asked for—and listed—the date of birth for each volunteer. Working back fifty years from 1904, he whittled away every woman born after 1860. The average life expectancy for females being 48.6 years, he was able to whittle away another 368 names, leaving him with just 23 possible suspects.

Next stop was a visit to the county registrar's office and his first significant obstacle of the day: the building was locked. A note on the door read: "Fair Hours: 8 a.m. - 1 p.m."

He glanced at his watch: 1:22. He did what any good detective would do under the circumstances. He took off his coat, wrapped it around his hand, and broke the window.

Once inside, he took his list and cross-referenced it against the county records to see if any of them had a child named Lucinda.

One did.

Obedience Everhardt.

Obedience was listed as having been married in 1857. Her husband, Titus, was shown as missing in action in 1865. He had been a passenger on the Sultana, which sank due to a boiler room explosion. The couple had one daughter, Lucinda, born 1859, with no recorded date of death. If she was still alive, Lucinda would be one of the lucky few who survived the typhoid epidemic that decimated much of the population of St. Louis during the summer of 1865.

Then Boyd looked at the address—*23 Hickory Street, E. St. Louis, Missouri*—and realized he knew the neighborhood all too well.

It was time for Detective Stormy Boyd to pay Mrs. Obedience Everhardt a long overdue visit.

* * *

Catfish pushed his way to the front of the line at the lost and found, irritating other fairgoers, and recounted the events of the previous day to the man behind the counter. People gasped in horror and waited silently with Catfish as the employee searched beneath the counter. When the man stood up with the Kodak Brownie in his hand, a cheer went up.

"Is there a place to get these pictures made?" Catfish asked.

"The Kodak Company has an exhibit," the man said.

"Yes," a woman said. "I had some pictures made yesterday. I'll take you."

Once there, Catfish went through the story again, but this time the young man in charge explained that his request—to have film made into picture prints while he waited—was simply impossible.

From the corner of the exhibit, a thin man in wire-rimmed glasses, sharply dressed in a gray double-breasted suit, stepped forward. "I heard your story, sir. If ever there was a time to do the impossible, I believe now is that time."

"Thank you, sir," Catfish said. "My daughter's name is Onyx, and I'll gladly pay..."

"There is no need for that, Mr. Webb," the man said extending his hand. "I wish only that you find your daughter, safe and sound, and perhaps speak kindly of Eastman Kodak to your friends. My name is George Eastman."

Another miracle, thought Catfish. Maybe there is a God after all.

It took less than an hour for the film to be developed and the prints to dry, at which time the young man brought them out and handed them to Catfish. Slowly, one at a time, the Cajun laid the photographic images on the counter.

He'd reached the final few photos and was losing hope. Only two more to go. And there it was... Geronimo. She had gone back.

With a single photo still to look at, Catfish took a breath, held it, and slid the picture of Geronimo to the side. *It was her, the gray-haired woman.*

There was no doubt in his mind.

The only thing left to do now was to head to the neighborhood where the girls had gone missing and later been found and show the photograph to as many people as he possibly could.

To his surprise, virtually everyone Catfish showed the picture to, recognized the woman, though none of them knew her name or where she lived until he showed the picture to the owner of a fabric store.

"That's Obedience Everhardt," the shop owner said.

Catfish's heart skipped a beat. "Do you happen to have her address?" he asked.

"Have it? I know it by heart," the shop owner said. "I mail her bill to her every week—*23 Hickory Street*—never pays on time."

"Is it far?" Catfish asked.

"23 Hickory Street is four blocks from where we're standing," the shop owner replied.

A third miracle.

Could there be a fourth?

FROM THE JOURNAL OF ONYX WEBB

The question I imagine you would want to have answered most is: why must a ghost kill to remain in the living plane?

The answer to that is simple: energy.

Energy, the thing of which all things in the universe are made...

Energy, the bane of my existence...

Energy, that which a ghost must have in order to move from the realm of the unseen—from a place of mist and shadows—to physical presence in the living plane.

This is not to say that I do so indiscriminately. To the contrary, I follow a strict code that allows me to justify what I do. A rule that permits me to take only those who are terminally ill, drug addicted beyond saving, the most heinous of criminals, and those hell-bent on taking their own lives.

It is a rule I have failed to abide by only once.

I had ventured away from the lighthouse for the purposes of finding energy. I was standing in the darkness, watching a young boy and girl sitting on the rocks by the ocean's edge. Even with the sound of waves crashing below I could hear every word they were saying.

The girl hated her parents. They controlled everything she did. The boy said he understood, his parents were the same, and hated them as well. She didn't think she could take another day, the girl had said. The boy said he'd had enough of his stupid life, too.

"Do you ever think about doing it?" the girl asked.

I leaned forward, listening for the word that would let me know they were mine for the taking.

"You mean ending it all?" he said.

"Suicide? I think about it all the time," the boy replied.

"How would we do it?" the girl said.

I snapped, unable to take any more. Rage boiled up inside of me, overwhelming me to the point of suffocation.

These ungrateful kids. How dare they? They had everything, yet appreciated none of it!

"You want to die that badly?" I thought as I moved steadily toward them. "Then I am willing to oblige."

The boy looked up and saw me standing over them. He stood, but before he could utter a single syllable I was on him, wrapping a hand behind his head and lowering my mouth over his.

The girl stood up but did not run. She remained there, frozen in a state of shock and fear, watching in horror. The boy went gray as I drained the life force from him, his lifeless body dropping limply to the rocks.

The girl found her legs and began to run.

She only got a few steps before I caught up...and it was over.

But as I stood there, basking in the glow of the silver moonlight on my now vibrantly colored skin, I knew something was wrong.

It was something I'd seen in their eyes—something that should not have been there.

It was fear.

They were scared, both of them, scared for their lives. They didn't want to die. They wanted to live.

And then I saw the cuts; multiple cuts on the inside of her arms. I didn't have to check the boy, I already knew. Their talk of suicide was nothing more than that - just talk - not true feelings, merely adolescent cries for help.

What had I done?

I was overcome with wave after wave of agonizing grief and unspeakable sorrow. All they wanted was for someone to care, for someone to love them. To live a full and happy life, just like everyone. Just like me.

In my rush to satisfy my lust for living, I had stolen theirs.

I dropped to the ground and began to vomit, but summoned nothing.

You see, ghosts do not eat.

Nor do we drink.

But trust me when I tell you, we feel regret.

SAVANNAH, GEORGIA
JUNE 3, 1979

Be calm," Quinn Cole told himself for the sixth time in the last two minutes. Yes, he'd given Juniper a one o'clock a.m. curfew, but it was prom night, after all.

But now—as he watched the small hand of the clock working its way toward 2:00 a.m.—he couldn't help but feel anxious. Wait another fifteen minutes, and if she's not home then...

Quinn blocked the thought out of his mind.

Juniper would walk in the door any moment.

But she didn't.

2:03 a.m.

Fortunately, Quinn had the foresight to get the boy's home telephone number from him before he'd left with Juniper. He dialed the number and waited as the phone rang again and again.

Just as Quinn was about to hang up, a groggy male voice answered. "Hello, who is this?"

"This is Quinn Cole. Your son took my sister to the prom tonight and..."

"Do you have any idea what time it is?" the man said.

"Yes, I do," said Quinn, "which is why I'm calling. My sister was supposed to be home by one o'clock, and she's not. Can I talk to your son?"

"No," the man responded. "He's staying at a friend's house. Hang on..." Quinn could hear the sound of muffled voices before he came back on the line. "My wife doesn't remember exactly which friend it was, but I wouldn't worry. I'm sure that, what's her name again?"

"Juniper," Quinn said, anger rising in his voice now. "Her name is Juniper, Juniper Cole. Are you telling me you let your son take my sister to the prom and you have no idea where he is or when he's coming home?"

"I'm not sure I like your tone," the man said.

"I want the names and phone numbers of all his friends and..."

"Screw off," the man said and hung up the phone.

Unbelievable, Quinn thought as he looked up at the clock...

2:17 a.m.

Quinn walked to the front room of the house and looked out the door at the driveway. He thought about calling the boy's father back but decided there was no point.

Then Quinn realized there was another option. He headed up the stairs, two at a time, and walked to his mother's bedroom.

The door was closed as usual. He lifted his hand to knock but changed his mind and continued down the hall to Juniper's room. He rarely went into her room, so he wasn't exactly sure where to look, but a small pink phone directory was lying in plain sight on the dresser.

He knew there were eight people in the group, which meant there were three other girls. One of the girls was someone he'd never heard of before and couldn't recall the name, but the other two were Juniper's best friends.

Quinn looked for the first girl's name, but it wasn't there. He took a deep breath and flipped forward to the "K" tab.

Thank God. Her number was there.

Quinn dialed the phone.

It rang only once, and a young girl answered. "Robbie, I told you to quit calling. You're going to wake my parents."

"Karen, this isn't Robbie. It's Quinn Cole, Juniper's brother."

"Oh, hey, Quinn, did Juniper get home okay?" Karen said.

Quinn's heart dropped. "What? Why would you ask that?"

"Because she wasn't there when the limo arrived," Karen said. "We wanted to wait for her but the guys wanted to split. So are you saying Juniper's not home yet?"

"Karen, when was the last time you saw Juniper?" Quinn asked.

"Gee, I don't really know," Karen said.

"Think, Karen. When's the last time you saw my sister?"

"Well, it was probably like about 10:30 or so. Her date was being like a jerk, pushing her to, you know, and she just walked off. I don't remember seeing her after that," Karen said. "I'm sorry, Quinn. I just assumed she'd gotten a ride with someone else."

Quinn hung up the phone and looked at his watch.

2:34 a.m.

The tightness in his stomach released and turned into a wave of fear that swept through him with a level of intensity beyond anything he imagined possible.

They say there's nothing worse for a parent than the loss of a child. Quinn wasn't Juniper's father, but he now knew it was true.

SAVANNAH, GEORGIA
JANUARY 23, 2010

Mika Flagler didn't give a damn about the old, musty building she was saving from the wrecking ball. All she knew was that being the event committee chairperson of the Restoring Savanna Foundation gave her a platform that placed her front and center in the *old money* circles that mattered to her most.

As the remaining heir to the fortune created by Henry Morrison Flagler—John D. Rockefeller's lesser-known partner and co-founder of Standard Oil—Mika's money was not only old, but she also had enough of it to make people sit up and take notice. $230 million worth, to be precise.

But who was counting?

Actually, she was.

Mika was tired of the letter *M*, as in million, having set her sights on the much prettier letter—*B*, as in billion.

That's where Koda Mulvaney came in.

She thought she had Koda reeled in. Then, two days after graduation from Syracuse, he'd run off to sow his wild oats.

That was nineteen months and twenty-three days ago, and Mika was tired of waiting.

*   *   *

Mika checked into her suite at the Forsyth Park Hotel—one of the oldest and most prestigious hotel destinations in Savannah, Georgia—a few minutes before ten in the morning.

She was right on schedule.

Mika required ample amount of time to complete her eleven-step beauty routine before the evening's event, which started promptly at 7:00 p.m. That gave her exactly nine hours, and she knew she would need every minute of it.

Step one: The facial she'd learned from her mother that involved mixing cold cream, honey, yogurt (plain, of course), aloe vera, and avocado in a portable blender, then applying the mask and allowing it to set for twenty minutes before removing it with cleansing facial pads.

Step two: Moisturizing her skin by placing two ounces of Elemis Pro-Collagen Cream in a portable electric warming tray (she'd tried placing the lotion on radiators and heating vents, always with disastrous results) and applying the warm liquid over every inch of skin from the chin down.

Step three: Rubbing a freshly cut lemon on all rough spots—especially elbows, knees, and heels—to both soften the skin and lighten dark areas.

Step four: Hand treatment, which involved combining a banana, two heaping tablespoons of cold cream, three drops of tea tree oil, and a teaspoon of olive oil in a blender, and applying liberally before slipping hands into a pair of rubber gloves and placing the gloved hands beneath a heating pad for fifteen minutes.

Step five: Exfoliating the skin by mixing one cup brown sugar, one cup raw oatmeal and one cup olive oil in a bowl—by hand, not in a blender—and then rubbing it on her skin in slow circles, then waiting thirty minutes before rinsing off in a cold shower.

Step six: The Shower Sauna. This involved placing several ounces of lavender-scented oil on the shower floor, then running the water at the hottest temperature possible for approximately fifteen minutes before reducing the heat slightly and stepping in.

Step seven: In-room body massage. Ten minutes prior, pour two cups of Evian water into electric teapot, bringing water to a boil then adding one cup of firmly packed rose petals to scent the air. Close shades. Conduct entire massage in dimly lit room. At conclusion, have masseuse roll table to edge of bed and slide in. Set alarm for one REM (ninety minutes).

Step eight: Shampoo hair with generous amount of Philip B's White Truffle Moisturizing Shampoo, followed by—ironically—coconut oil conditioner from Trader Joes.

Step nine: Hair.

Step ten: Nails.

Step eleven: Make-up.

Mika leaned forward and peered at her reflection in the vanity mirror as she applied a generous amount of Guerlain Diamond-Studded Lipstick, Color No. 850 Moka Shake. The lipstick itself was not expensive, available in most stores for $8—but the lipstick holder was made of eighteen-karat gold and adorned with 199 diamonds weighing 2.2 karats—with a price tag of $62,000.

In Mika's opinion, there was no one on the planet who possessed as much taste as she.

There was a dog barking in the hallway. Mika looked at her watch and smiled. Attention to detail combined with rigid planning had put her a full six minutes ahead of schedule.

Even though she knew it wasn't necessary, Mika took one last look in the mirror.

Perfect.

She opened the door and found her assistant standing there, leash in hand, as expected.

"Someone called the office and..."

Mika ignored him and placed her attention solely on the dog—a half-Great Dane, half-Newfoundland mix-breed—that stood six feet four on his hind legs and weighed in at 245 pounds.

His name was Tiny.

"There's my baby!" Mika said in playful, baby-talk voice. "Did you have a nice day at the doggy day spa?"

"I'm not sure if we can take him there again," the assistant said. "He started humping a miniature poodle and some of the regular customers complained that he frightened them."

"Did you hump a poodle?" Mika said to the dog. "Did you? Did you? What a good boy you are!"

Mika took the leash from the assistant.

"How do I look?" she asked.

"Wow! You look really..."

There was no need for the assistant to finish the sentence—Mika was already halfway down the hall.

*   *   *

"So this is how the other half lives," Koda Mulvaney said as he and Dane entered their room. The accommodations—a standard room with two queen-sized beds and a single bathroom—had been arranged by the MPI travel department per company guidelines.

"Trust me, the other half would give their right arm to stay in a place like this," Dane said. "I should know—I *am* the other half."

Even with the small digs, Koda was relieved to get out of Orlando for a few days. "I never thought I would ever have to ask anyone this question," Koda said, "but which bed do you want?"

Dane laughed.

For Dane, the last two years had been an experience beyond his wildest dreams. And he'd never forgotten his upstate New York roots, acutely aware that the day would come when he'd be forced to return to the real world.

But for Koda, things were different—*very different*. He'd lived in a bubble of wealth, celebrity, and entitlement his entire life. And now that bubble had burst.

To everyone's surprise, Koda had—after those first few days of adjustment—gotten down to work and impressed co-workers with his intelligence and natural business skills. Skills he'd never been challenged to use before now.

Koda looked at his watch. "We better get going."

*   *   *

"You sure they got your measurements?" Koda called from the bathroom, attempting to tie his bowtie for the fourth time. *It's just like tying your shoe,* his father had said, but for whatever reason he couldn't get the hang of it.

"Yeah, I faxed it on Thursday." Dane yelled back, wearing only his boxer shorts and black over-the-calf socks. "They said..."

There was a knock on the door. "In the nick of time," Dane said as he walked to the door and pulled it open.

It wasn't his tux.

It was Mika Flagler.

ST. LOUIS, MISSOURI
AUGUST 7, 1904

Six-year-old Onyx Webb had never seen anyone tied to a chair before. She had also never seen anyone die. Now she was about to see both.

"Help me!" pleaded the young girl again. "Please!"

Onyx wanted to help—knew she should help—but she simply couldn't. Not only had she been told not to, she found herself paralyzed with fear and unable to move a muscle.

"We've got to get out of here!" said the girl with more urgency. "You've got to..."

"She told me not to or I couldn't go home," said Onyx, cutting her off.

"Home? You're not going home," Katherine said. She pulled, the ropes digging into her wrists, blood seeping from her torn skin, tears streaming down her face. "None of us goes home, not ever!"

Onyx began to cry. "I... don't... understand," she said, choking the words. "Who... who is... she?"

"That doesn't matter right now!" shouted Katherine. "What matters now is that you help get us out of here!"

"Don't yell at me! I didn't do anything wrong, I... just..."

Katherine stopped tugging on the ropes and looked at Onyx. "I'm sorry, you're right," she said in a calming voice. "What's your name?"

"It's Onyx."

"Onyx," Katherine said, nodding and forcing a smile. "That's a real nice name, pretty."

"My other name is Webb," Onyx said, "with two letter *b*'s on the end."

"Listen to me, Onyx Webb with two letter *b*'s... my name is Katherine, and I need your help. I need you to trust me. Can you do that?"

"Okay," Onyx said.

"Good. I need you to look around and find something to cut this rope with," Katherine said.

"Something sharp, right?" Onyx said.

"Yes, something sharp, Onyx. There's got to be something— a knife, a piece of metal maybe. Back there, under the stairs, look over there."

Onyx made her way toward where Katherine directed her when she spotted the cabinet. "What's in here?" Onyx asked.

"No, not the drawers," Katherine said.

"What's in them?" asked Onyx.

"Nothing, Onyx," Katherine snapped, but Onyx had already moved toward the cabinet. "They're empty, Onyx, trust me."

Onyx pulled on the top drawer, leaned forward and looked inside. "Masks!" she exclaimed, reaching in and holding one up for Katherine to see. "Masks, like at Halloween." Onyx placed the mask over her own face. "It fits," she said, looking through the eye slits at Katherine who had hung her head and was weeping uncontrollably.

Onyx lowered the mask. "What's the matter? They're just masks," she said. Then she looked in the drawer again and saw the entire row of faces staring back at her. Young girls faces. "They all look alike," said Onyx almost to herself. "They all look like..."

Onyx stopped in mid-sentence and looked at Katherine.

"Us," Katherine said. "They all look like us, like you and me. She makes a mask of each girl, Onyx," Katherine said.

"What girls?" Onyx asked.

"The girls she takes and keeps here in this room, the girls she took before she took me, and now you."

"They all have the same scar just like you have," Onyx said. "On their mouths..."

"She does it to us. She does it to make us look like her dead daughter, Lucinda," said Katherine.

"Why?" Onyx asked.

"Because she's crazy!" Katherine screamed, instantly regretting the outburst as Onyx began to cry. "I'm sorry, Onyx, I'm sorry—I know you're scared. I'm scared too—but you've got to help me find something to cut these ropes. Please, Onyx."

Onyx nodded, placed the mask back in the drawer and began searching under the stairs. "Here! What about this?" she said, holding up a jagged piece of glass.

"Yes!" Katherine said. "Yes, bring it here!"

Onyx started across the room toward Katherine then stopped dead in her tracks as light streamed into the basement from the top of the stairwell. "Oh, God," said Katherine as the sound of feet could be heard on the wooden stairs above them.

Obedience.

"Happy Birthday to you..." she said in a sing-song voice as she slowly came down the stairs.

"Oh God, oh God..."

"Happy Birthday to you..."

"Oh God, oh God, oh God..."

"Happy Birth-day, dear Lu-cin-da..."

"No, no, no, no, no..." Katherine pleaded.

"Happy Birthday... to you."

Katherine Keane looked up to see the gray-haired woman standing there, birthday cake in one hand and a pair of pliers in the other. "We'll get to you in a minute, dear," the old woman said to Katherine. "But first we have to make Lucinda pretty," she said, turning her sights on Onyx.

"My name isn't Lucinda, its Onyx—Onyx Webb. And you're not my mom!"

"Do you want to have your cake now?" Obedience asked. "No, I say we make you pretty first." The old woman walked over, closed the drawer with the masks and set the cake on the cabinet.

"Run, Onyx!" Katherine screamed. "Up the stairs! Try the door! Try the door!"

"I think we've had just about enough out of you," Obedience said, pulling a rag from the pocket of her dress. She reached down and grabbed Katherine's face, trying to force her mouth open.

"Leave her alone!" Onyx shouted. "Katherine is my friend!"

"Katherine?" Obedience said. "Is that what she said her name was?"

"Yes," Onyx said. "Her name is..."

"Her name was Lucinda, but not anymore—she's too old, too big," Obedience said.

"Onyx, run!" Katherine screamed again. "The door!"

Obedience attempted again to force the rag in Katherine's mouth. Katherine clenched her teeth, shaking her head from side to side. Obedience slammed her fist hard into Katherine's stomach. Katherine let out a gasp, and Obedience jammed the rag deep into her throat.

Onyx darted up the stairs but when she reached the landing she found the big wooden door was locked. Onyx peered down the stairwell at the old woman who she now *knew* was crazy, just like Katherine had said. "I want my dad," Onyx cried. "I want my daddy!"

Obedience walked casually to the bottom of the stairs, looked up. "Don't worry, daddy is on his way. The war is over and he'll be here any day now. Now, please, it's getting late, and we have to make you pretty." The old woman held up the pliers. "You have too many teeth to be my Lucinda, some of them have simply got to go."

The old woman started up the stairs toward Onyx.

"Don't you remember, Lucinda? You were roller skating, and you fell, knocked three teeth right out. But daddy said you were still his pretty girl—his pretty, pretty, girl—even with that nasty scar. But don't worry, momma's going to help you be pretty again," Obedience said, waving the pliers in her hand.

Onyx opened her mouth to scream.

SAVANNAH, GEORGIA
JUNE 3, 1979

Quinn Cole was going out of his mind.

2:39 a.m.

His call to the Savannah P.D. was dismissed out-of-hand since the police received an average of thirty-six calls every Friday and Saturday night during prom season from panicked parents whose sons or daughters failed to come home as promised. "And do you know how many of those kids show up over the next few hours?" the desk sergeant asked. "Thirty-six, Mr. Cole, each and every one of 'em."

"This is different. Juniper would never..."

"...blah, blah, blah, I heard it all before. By the way, why is it that you're the one calling us? Where are your parents?"

Quinn ignored the question because the reason didn't matter. "How long do I have to wait until you do something? And don't give me any standard TV show bullshit about her having to be missing 24 hours."

"I'll tell you what," the desk sergeant said. "I'm on till 8:00 a.m. If your sister hasn't shown by 6:00 a.m., call me and I'll see what we can do, but trust me—she'll come walking through the door before that, saying how sorry she is, how she lost track of time, blah, blah, blah."

6:01 a.m.

Quinn Cole pushed through the glass doors of the Savannah Police Department and didn't have to look very hard for the desk sergeant since he was the only officer in the place.

"My name is Quinn Cole, Sergeant. We talked a few hours ago about my sister Juniper. It is 6:02 a.m. and she's not back yet, so what do we do now?"

8:41 a.m.

A man who appeared to be in his mid-fifties, his hair turning gray at the temples to match his light gray suit, walked toward

Quinn with a cup of coffee in one hand and a half-eaten bagel in the other.

"You Cole?" the man asked. Quinn nodded and stood up.

"Come with me," the man said.

The man led Quinn to an elevator door. "Hit the up button, huh? Damn thing is brand new. Cost the department $26,000 to put in, if you can believe that. And it's slower than shit."

The man was right. Quinn had never been on a slower elevator in his life and couldn't understand why they hadn't just taken the stairs.

They arrived at a typical gray metal desk against the far wall of the room. The combination of the name plate on the desk—which read Det. Leopold Igler—and the bagel made Quinn assume the detective was Jewish.

Not that it mattered.

"Detective, I'm here because..."

"First things first, call me Leo," Leo Igler said as he lowered his five-foot-eleven frame into his swivel chair.

Quinn said nothing. He didn't need a Leo, he needed a detective.

Leo rocked back in his chair. "Okay, have it your way. Let's start with the obvious. Where are your parents?"

"What do my parents have to—?"

"Humor me, okay kid? I'm not asking the question to waste time, I'm asking it to *save* time," Leo said. "See, I've been a detective for going on twenty-six years now, and never in all that time has the brother come in to report a missing sister—it's always the parents. So, what's the story with your parents?"

"My father is in California, and my mother is sick," Quinn said. "Okay?"

"No, kid, half answers are not okay," Leo said. "What you left out, what you failed to say, is *why* your father is in California and why your mother's not."

Quinn seethed.

Leo waited.

"My father left my mother for another woman, and my mother is a drunk who doesn't get out of bed or go out of the house unless it's to buy a case of Boone's Farm," Quinn said. "Is that a complete enough answer for you, detective?"

Leo nodded. "Yeah, now we're getting somewhere."

"Getting somewhere?" Quinn said. "We're getting nowhere. We're going in circles. What do—?"

"Your sister is a runaway," Leo said, cutting Quinn off. "I've seen it a thousand times with kids who've got problems at home. My best guess? She'll be back in a few days."

Quinn shot to his feet. "Jesus Christ! What in the hell is it with you people?" he shouted loudly enough that everyone in the room stopped what they were doing and stared. "First I'm told she'll be back in a few hours. Now you're telling me she'll be back in a few days? What's next? Is there some other department you send me to next where I'm told she'll be back in just a few years? Isn't there anyone... anyone...?"

Leo stood and put his arm around Quinn's shoulders as the tears morphed into choking sobs. "Sit down, kid, okay?" Leo said. "Take a seat, and we'll work this thing through together. Okay?"

As Quinn regained his composure, Leo pulled a notepad from his desk drawer and a pen from the inside pocket of his suit jacket. Leo clicked the back of the pen with his thumb.

"Okay, Quinn," Leo said. "Tell me about your sister."

Quinn told him everything he could think of that might be of help. And though he didn't think all that much had been accomplished, Quinn felt that someone was finally listening to him.

"Anyone your sister ever dated who ever got violent with her or had anger issues?" Leo asked. "Anyone who may have made comments of a sexual nature, anyone who—"

It only lasted a fraction of a second, but Leo saw something on Quinn's face—a brief flash of recognition in the young man's eyes—that made Leo think he'd hit on something.

"What is it?" Leo asked.

Quinn shook his head. "No, it's nothing."

"Sometimes nothing turns into something," Leo said.

Leo remained silent and watched Quinn thinking.

About Wyatt Scrogger...

The pick-up lines and sexual innuendos...

The comment about Juniper's breasts...

The hug that lasted just a bit too long...

"Come on, kid," Leo said. "Spit it out."

*   *   *

2:19 p.m.

Leo spent a few hours digesting what Quinn Cole had told him about his friend. All-in-all the Scrogger lead was pretty thin. Comments and jokes didn't amount to much on their own.

3:34 p.m.

A little over an hour later, a uniformed cop dropped a file and a stack of newspaper clippings on Leo's desk. Leo slid on his reading glasses and flipped through the stack.

Juniper Cole had never been in trouble.

Juniper Cole was a straight A student.

Juniper Cole was on the high school chess team.

And then Leo read the next line:

Juniper Cole was a child piano prodigy who'd appeared on Johnny Carson's Tonight Show and performed at Carnegie Hall.

Leo realized he'd been wrong.

She hadn't run away. Hell, this girl was a local celebrity.

And the Savannah PD had reacted too slowly.

He had reacted too slowly.

Leo glanced at his watch. Assuming someone had taken the Cole girl around midnight the night before—and Leo's gut now told him that someone had—he was fifteen hours behind.

SAVANNAH, GEORGIA
JANUARY 23, 2010

"My, my," Mika Flagler said from the hallway, looking at Dane, who was standing there in nothing but his boxer shorts. "Is that a lacrosse stick in your pants or are you just happy to see me?"

"Walking dogs to make a few extra bucks?" Dane said eyeing the giant hound.

"This is Tiny," Mika said, handing the dog leash to Dane. "You two should get along nicely. He's a Great Dane, like you," Mika added, pushing past Dane into the small room.

"You're not planning on wearing that to the dinner, are you?" Dane asked. The silk garment looked as if someone had stitched a dozen enormous Monarch butterfly wings together, the wings fluttering in the breeze as she walked.

"It's Stella McCartney's. I stole it from her suite at the St. Regis in New York after Paul's concert at MSG—don't tell her it was me. Where's Koda?"

"Working on his bowtie," Dane said.

"Oh, God, we'll never get out of here," Mika said, glancing around the room. "Isn't that cute, you each have your own little beds. Remind me to have the concierge send up a couple pairs of Spider-Man pajamas."

Koda turned off the bathroom light and stepped into the room. He stopped dead when he saw the dog. "What in the hell is that?"

"This is Tiny," Mika said. "I got him after I saw you on the red carpet in Cannes with that troll, Paris, and that stupid Chihuahua she had stuffed in her purse like an emergency bag of Cheetos."

"You named him Tiny?" Koda said.

"You know me, I don't do small," Mika said. "Now come here and give me a kiss."

Koda stepped forward and leaned in to kiss her, but as soon as he did Mika slapped him hard across the face.

Koda rubbed his cheek. "Feel better?"

"You have no idea." Mika took a step back. "So, what do you think of my dress?"

Koda looked Mika up and down. "Garish, as usual."

Mika turned and grabbed the leash from Dane. "Let's go, I'm starved."

"We're waiting for Dane's tux," Koda said.

"Dane's a big boy, he can dress himself," Mika said. "You know how much I hate to be late."

*　　*　　*

The ballroom was decorated entirely in gold and white, with forty round tables set for eight each, an array of food stations placed strategically around the room serving lobster, caviar, shrimp, prime rib, crepes, sushi, wheat grass shooters, and over a hundred kinds of cheese.

Savannah's most-notable citizens nibbled at their food, renewed relationships and toasted each other's wealth from oversized crystal glasses filled with *Petrus Pomerol* Chardonnay and *Screaming Eagle* Cabernet.

Every inch of the room was flawlessly executed and breathtakingly beautiful. Mika had seen to it personally, refusing to delegate a single decision. Of course, at $25,000 a plate, it had to be—especially when almost any of the attendees could pull out a checkbook and buy the entire hotel simply on a whim.

Koda and Mika stood near the doorway at the front of the room, near the stage, waiting to be introduced. Koda glanced up and saw hundreds of large Monarch butterflies hanging from the ceiling from wires—their wings fluttering in the subtle breeze that came from two large ceiling fans—and knew instantly that Mika's dress had not been chosen by accident.

Everything Mika Flagler did was part of a grand plan—a plan that, in the end, would serve her personal wants and needs. It was something Koda simultaneously admired and despised about her.

*   *   *

The presenter on the stage was a dead-ringer for Colonel Sanders, known around Charleston and Savannah as *The Southern Gentleman*—a moniker he'd bestowed upon himself twenty years earlier. He'd become a mini-celebrity of sorts, serving as the Master of Ceremony at various events.

Koda and Mika waited in the wings while The Southern Gentleman worked the audience with his unique presentation, reminding members of the audience of days gone by, working them for applause and laughs:

> *While we're restoring Savannah's buildings to their previous states of wonder l believe we should be equally focused on restoring Savannah's culture—a culture that, if we are not careful, will eventually go the way of the dodo bird and the drive-in theater.*

> *I cite, as an example, the nearly extinct species referred to by biologists as "Southern-ous Gentlemen-ous"—a species that has sadly become little more than a memory in the South—a dying idea, or should I say, dying ideal. I say this out of a desire for self-preservation, for I am a southern gentleman!*

> *And what is it that defines a person of my breed?*

> *A southern gentleman knows how to make a mint julep and a whisky sour when someone asks.*

> *A southern gentleman wears a hat, even indoors, though never at the table. May I add, gentleman, that a wide-brimmed straw hat is never out of style, nor is a pair of highly polished spats.*

> *A southern gentleman never underestimates the triple threat of new ideas, aged Scotch, and old money.*

A southern gentleman knows how to eat and feels no trepidation when it comes to asking for seconds.

A southern gentleman will gladly offer you the shirt off his back, even if it's his last.

A southern gentleman always greets a lady with a devilish smile on his face that never lets you know exactly what he's thinkin'. Sometimes a devilish smile is just a smile, and sometimes it's worn to hide the real person. It is your job, ladies, to figure out which is which.

Speaking of the other sex, when it comes to women, life for a southern gentleman is a race: A race to anticipate her needs... a race to open a lady's door... a race to pull out a lady's chair... a race to take a lady's coat... a race to throw your white Armani dinner jacket over a puddle to ensure her comfortable passage.

Okay, maybe I went a bit too far with that last one.

'Course, we southern gentlemen do have—despite all our positive traits and social graces—a few, shall I say, shortcomings.

We like to hunt and fish—and hunt and fish—and sometimes we lose track of time and forget to come home as promised.

The ladies in the audience laughed—some of them a bit too loudly—the wine clearly having its intended effect now, as The Southern Gentleman pushed on:

Our strong opinions can cause us to come off as a bit too passionate at times, and we're known to let our tempers get the best of us. And, when someone wrongs us, we don't always wait for the courts to right a wrong—we right it ourselves.

"That was interesting," Koda said.

"They love him," Mika said. "The man says everything they believe, but don't have the courage to say out loud."

"Well, he's pretty creepy if you ask me," Koda said as the Southern Gentleman drawled on:

Now, I'm not sayin' any of these traits are good, or even acceptable, in today's society. I'm just pointing out the truth—that we Southern Gentleman are what we are— and if you're fixin' to hitch yourself to a true southern gent, make sure you like the old dog just the way he is, 'cause we aren't going to learn any new tricks, no matter how much you beg and plead.

Colonel Sanders was a true southern gentleman... as were Robert E. Lee, Johnny Cash, Rhett Butler and Elvis.

But where have all the Rhett Butler's gone? For that matter, where have all the Scarlett O'Hara's gone?

Ladies and gentlemen, I end my time with you tonight by simply making the point that—here, in our beloved South—tourists will come and tourists will go, but true southern gentlemen and true southern belles... are... fahevah!

The band began playing *Dixie* and the room exploded with applause.

Mika turned to Koda and said, "Are you ready?"

"Yeah, I guess," Koda said.

"You guess?" Mika said sharply. "This is the most important event of my year, Koda, do you understand that? I need you to be focused. I need you to be on."

The applause died away and The Southern Gentleman began to introduce Koda and Mika:

Ladies and gentlemen, it is my extreme honor to introduce your hosts for this evening's event. Representing Mulvaney Properties International—and this year's "People" magazine Sexiest Man Alive—Mr. Koda Mulvaney...

And the Chairperson and driving force behind the Restoring Savannah Foundation, Ms. Mika Flagler, and her dog, Tiny. Oh, and it says here I'm supposed to point out that Mr. Mulvaney is the dog to Ms. Flagler's left.

As the audience roared with laughter, Mika turned and leveled a stare at Koda. "I need you to give the speech of your life, Koda—*I need you to be Tony Robbins.*"

He wasn't.

* * *

The general assessment of Koda Mulvaney's performance from the stage included the words flat, lifeless, monotone, passionless and boring—*and those were the good parts.*

Mika was beyond furious.

Koda went straight to the bar, with Dane close behind. "It wasn't that bad," Dane said when he finally caught up.

"Tito's rocks," Koda said to the bartender, ignoring Dane.

When the bartender returned with the drink, Koda took it straight from the man's hand and downed it with several quick gulps, then signaled for another.

Dane knew exactly where things were headed.

Dane had seen things like this play out hundreds of times over the last four years, back at school in Syracuse—and more recently—during their travels around the world.

It was never good.

Koda and Dane stood side by side at the bar, and Dane could hear Koda taking deep breaths as if he were about to hyperventilate—something else Dane had seen happen a number of times. "You want me to find a bag?" Dane asked.

"Just give me some space," Koda said.

"So the speech wasn't that good, so what?" Dane said, not backing off. "And screw Mika, okay? She doesn't really care about you, all she cares about is being socialite of the year."

The bartender returned and set Koda's second drink on a napkin. "You know that's not the answer, right?" Dane said as Koda reached for the drink.

"Are you my mother all of a sudden?" Koda said. "Oh, I forgot—you can't be my mother. My mother abandoned me when I was six. You must be my hired nanny."

Koda picked up the drink, but as he raised it to his lips Dane slapped the glass out of his hand, sending vodka and ice all over the bar.

At that moment, Koda did the last thing either of them would have ever expected—he turned and punched Dane in the mouth, sending him reeling into the man behind him.

The entire bar went quiet.

Dane reached up and touched his face, examined the blood on his hand.

"You want me to call the police?" the bartender asked. "Technically, that's assault."

"Yeah, I'm a witness," the man behind Dane said.

"No, don't," Dane said. "He's got enough problems already."

ST. LOUIS, MISSOURI
AUGUST 6, 1904

etective Stormy Boyd walked passed 23 Hickory Street for the second time, surveying the best way to approach the building; a two story, single-family dwelling built between 1830 and 1850.

He had been inside homes like this before and knew the front door led to a sitting room, the door in the rear lead to the cellar. All the homes built during that period had storm cellars, especially those in the middle of tornado alley, which is how "Stormy" Boyd had gotten his nickname.

According to Stormy's parents, he'd been conceived in a storm cellar during the devastating tornado of 1854. It was his belief that if Obedience Everhardt was holding Onyx Webb, it would be in the cellar.

Stormy Boyd made his way to the alley where he discovered Catfish Webb. "Looks like I underestimated you, Mr. Webb," Stormy said.

"And I you, detective," Catfish said. "How do you know she be the one?"

"I followed the button, and it led me here," Stormy said. "And you?"

"Her photo was on Onyx's camera," Catfish said.

Boyd motioned to the back door. "Probably a stairway just inside here leading down to the cellar," Boyd said.

"How do you know there's a cellar?" Catfish asked.

"We're in tornado alley, Mr. Webb," Boyd said. "Every house built here after 1854 has a storm cellar."

"Your call, detective," Catfish said. "Where I come from, all we got is houseboats and shacks, so I trust your judgment."

"So how'd you know to come to the back of the house?" Boyd asked.

"When you go to catch a gator, you always sneak up on it from behind."

Stormy nodded at the logic. "You got another plan?"

"No," Catfish said, pulling the Landers & Clark hunting knife from its sheath. "But I got this."

"And I've got this," Stormy said, but before he could even pull the Colt police revolver from his shoulder holster, they heard a scream from just inside the house.

"Onyx!" Catfish yelled.

Stormy stepped forward and kicked the door next to the lock as he'd been trained. The door did not open.

"Stand aside," Catfish said. He took a step back, then threw his large frame into the door with all his might—once, twice—and on the third time the door splintered and gave way.

Catfish was the first in.

"Daddy!" Onyx screamed.

Catfish grabbed Onyx and pulled her into his arms as Stormy Boyd—gun drawn now—followed directly behind him.

Obedience saw the gun and stopped dead in her tracks.

In a fit of uncontrolled rage, Obedience charged up the last few steps toward them, the pliers in her outstretched hand.

Stormy Boyd assumed she had a gun.

The sound of the blast echoed off the walls as the bullet caught Obedience Everhardt on the right shoulder, sending her flying backward, head over heels, tumbling down the stairs to the cellar floor below.

As Catfish tended to Onyx, Stormy Boyd made his way down the stairwell to where Obedience laid motionless and checked for a pulse.

Unbelievably, the woman was still alive.

Then Onyx screamed. "Katherine! Katherine!"

It was only then that the two men spotted Katherine Keane at the far end of the cellar, tied naked in the wooden chair.

Stormy raced over to the girl, lifted her head and slapped her cheek. There was no response. He pulled the rag from her mouth, placed his ear near her mouth. She was not breathing.

She was still.

She was blue.

She was lifeless.

Stormy looked up, shook his head. "She's gone."

"No!" Onyx screamed. "Do something! Make Katherine okay! Make her live!"

Stormy knew it was hopeless, but there was a theory within the medical community—though still unproven—that life could be breathed into someone by placing your mouth over theirs, and the human heart could be restarted by pressing on it with your hand. He had no idea if either theory were true, but there was nothing left to try, and nothing to lose.

"Help me get her out of the chair."

Catfish used his knife to cut the ropes and placed Katherine on the floor as Stormy Boyd pushed on the lifeless girl's chest...

And then again, a bit harder this time...

And then again.

There was no response. He leaned down and placed his mouth over hers, and pushed a breath of air into her chest.

That's when Onyx noticed a gray mist hovering in the air. The mist rose higher and higher, pausing near where she was standing at the top of the stairs.

Somehow Onyx knew it was Katherine, her spirit, watching the scene unfolding below.

Stormy leaned back and shook his head.

It was useless.

"No!" Onyx screamed. "Try again!"

What more can I do? Stormy thought. *If I could give my life so that this one could live, I would. God, take me if you want, take me so this one can live. She is so very young, and I have lived my years. Please, God, take me!*

The searing pain hit Boyd's chest with the force of a lightning bolt, and before he could so much as utter a word, he dropped to the floor beside Katherine.

Katherine's eyes snapped open. She sat upright and looked down at Stormy Boyd, then watched as the detective's spirit rose from his body in a grayish mist—higher and higher in the air—until his spirit was at the top of the landing where Onyx stood.

Then, as if in a burst of cosmic energy, he flew out the open door and into the light of day.

"Did you see him, Daddy?" Onyx asked.

"See what, Jitterbug?" Catfish said. "I didn't see anything, child."

"He went to heaven, Daddy," Onyx said. "He went to heaven where Mama is."

* * *

The other thing neither Catfish or Onyx had seen during all the commotion was Obedience Everhardt—her hand pressed over the bullet wound in her shoulder, careful to avoid leaving a trail of blood—and crawling quietly across the floor toward the secret compartment.

Titus had installed it when the house was built, just in case Obedience and Lucinda were ever in peril and needed a place to hide.

"Should you one day discover you have both light and darkness inside you, do not despair. We all do. The only thing that **matters** is which you choose to act on."

The 31 Immutable Matters
of Life & Death

Episode 2
The Girl in the Mirror

This Episode Dedicated to:

Jack Canfield

For inviting us into your home and sharing your wisdom, which has—over the past 20-plus years—enriched our minds and filled our hearts with the endless possibilities life provides to us all.

And to the following
Onyx Webb "Super Fans"...

Katie & Javier Calderon
Tammy Pugh
Tom Schaff

Written primarily to music by:

Fun

In particular...

"All the Pretty Girls"
"Be Calm"
"The Gambler"
"Stars"
"Carry On"
"Some Nights"

SAVANNAH, GEORGIA
JUNE 3, 1979

Juniper couldn't believe she'd let herself get stranded in the park. All the limos were gone. All she could think about was how angry her brother, Quinn, was going to be.

Then she heard a man's voice from behind her.

Juniper Cole turned and saw a man sitting in a wheelchair on the sidewalk.

He looked to be in his early thirties and a little heavy in the middle, like one of her father's friends who had what they called a beer belly. His stomach was accentuated even more by the tan vest he was wearing, which had lots of pockets all over it, like something she imagined a person would wear on an African safari.

In his hand was what looked to be an expensive camera, with a long, telescopic lens.

"I saw you, over at the fountain," the man said. "*In* the fountain, actually."

"Yes, I was just—"

"No need to explain anything to me, little lady," the man said. "If I had the use of my legs still, I'd be jumping in fountains and dancing around all the time."

Juniper laughed, let out a breath.

There was nothing to fear.

She could outrun the man if she wanted to, even in her prom dress.

"Looks like you might have missed your ride," he said.

"Yeah, I guess I did. Dumb, huh?" Juniper said.

"Well, you're in luck," the man said. "Because my van is sitting right there. If you want, I'd be pleased to drive you home."

"Oh, no, that's okay," Juniper said. "I'll just go across the street and call my brother, but thanks."

"That would probably be best," the man in the wheelchair replied. "But, when your brother gets here, please let him know the Savannah P.D. was doing its job to protect and serve."

"You're with the Savannah Police Department?" Juniper asked.

The man reached inside one of the pockets of his vest and pulled out a wallet and flipped it open. "I'm not a cop, actually. I'm the department photographer. That's what I was doing out here tonight, taking photos of the fountain, so beautiful at night."

Juniper looked down at her watch to see it was 12:20. If she called Quinn, he'd have to get dressed and drive down to get her.

She knew how disappointed he'd be.

Or she could simply accept the offer and be just a few minutes late. Besides, what harm could come from accepting?

He worked for the police.

SAVANNAH, GEORGIA
JANUARY 23, 2010

Koda felt sick, and the six double vodkas had nothing to do with it.

It was having punched his best friend, and over what? Because Dane cared about him? God, he was a total shit.

Koda raised his hand, signaling to the bartender to bring another drink.

This was a different bar and a different bartender, over in the older section of the property, since it had become clear that Koda was *persona non grata* in the cocktail lounge in the hotel lobby.

Koda drained the final drops from his drink as a tuxedoed lounge performer began another set of old Sinatra tunes on the piano behind him.

"You got a bathroom?" Koda slurred.

"Take a left at the end of the hall. You can't miss it.

*   *   *

It was not until he was on his way back to the piano lounge from the men's restroom that Koda saw the mirror.

Six feet tall, the mirror was extraordinarily ornate, especially the details around the outer edges, which were trimmed in colors of gold and silver.

As he stood there—swaying slightly from side to side from the alcohol that had made its way through his bloodstream—Koda felt something stir inside him.

A memory.

A memory of the morning he'd woken up, at the age of six, to discover his mother had left the night before and had not returned.

She never would.

She hadn't even said good-bye or even left a note explaining where she'd gone.

They say that most kids end up blaming themselves for their parents' divorce, but that was something Koda had never done. He knew it wasn't his fault.

It was his father's fault.

Bruce.

She had left because his father had put his career and making money first, and his family second.

And he still hated his father for it.

This, more than anything, was at the root of their rocky relationship.

The therapist said it was his mother's abandonment that was the cause of Koda's recurring nightmares—or more accurately—the same nightmare he'd had over and over throughout his life. The one where he found himself wandering the house the night she'd gone missing, ending up in the basement, following her voice as she called for help.

Bruce Mulvaney had insisted that Koda's mother would never have left them like that, that something had happened to her.

He went so far as to offer a $1 million reward to anyone who provided information that led to her safe return.

There were the calls from an array of crackpots, of course—nut jobs claiming they'd seen her, some even claiming they had taken her—but nothing ever panned out. And it never would.

His father had even gotten the FBI involved when it was discovered several weeks later that his mother's Mercedes Benz was found parked at the curb outside a Savannah dive bar, a place called Pinkie Masters. But nothing ever came of it.

Eventually, everyone assumed nothing nefarious had happened to his mother, including the FBI. Bruce Mulvaney's beautiful wife had just finally gotten fed up enough to leave the bastard.

Koda looked up at the mirror and remembered the one thing his mother did leave.

A photograph.

It was a picture his father had taken of Koda and his mother, sitting on a swing in Charleston, South Carolina, about a month before she'd left.

Just the two of them, sitting side by side—swinging back and forth on a beautiful sunny day—smiling, happy, together.

His mother had left the picture taped to the mirror in Koda's bedroom, nothing written on it.

Without thinking, Koda reached toward the mirror—just as he'd reached out to take the photo off the mirror when he was six—and just as his finger touched the glass...

He saw her.

A girl.

She was standing opposite him as if a mirror image, her arm reaching out toward the mirror just as Koda's was, her fingers touching the mirror in the exact place his fingers were touching.

Koda jumped back, shocked at what he was seeing.

But the girl didn't move.

She just stood there looking at him as if fascinated at what she was seeing.

Then she simply faded away.

*   *   *

Though the Restoring Savannah banquet had formally come to an end, the evening was far from over. In fact, as far as Mika Flagler was concerned, the most important part of the evening was just getting started—a tradition that had become known as "Black Midnight" among the select-few committee members and high-value donors lucky enough to be invited to join her.

It started as an impromptu gathering, three years earlier when Mika invited a few people to share a bottle of rare cognac given to her by a friend. But, as is prone to happen in situations such as these, word got out and Mika suddenly found herself overwhelmed with requests to be included the next time. Mika saw the situation for what it was—another opportunity to place herself at the center of power.

The name "Black Midnight" came from the name of the cognac being shared—a Remy Martin "Black Pearl" Louis XIII cognac, one of the most expensive liqueurs in the world—at $50,000 per bottle. Packaged in a black-crystal Baccarat decanter, the cognac had been aged 115 years—with only 786 decanters produced.

Mika had called in numerous favors and managed to score six bottles. If this were not enough, Mika had the cognac served in black crystal nocturnes, mouth-blown by Swarovski's top glassmaker in Austria.

The ante was upped the following year when Mika added one of the most expensive cigars in the world—a hand-rolled Honduran cigar called the Gurkha Black Dragon. Production of the 8½-inch, fifty-two-gauge smoke—made from the rarest tobaccos from across the globe—was limited to just one-hundred hand-carved boxes per year, with a hundred cigars in each. She had managed to get her hands on two boxes at $115,000 each.

Because Mika restricted attendance to just eighteen people, demand to be included had reached a fever pitch, exactly what she'd intended. This year there was a last- minute opening—Koda Mulvaney had been ceremoniously uninvited after embarrassing himself—and Mika—with his atrocious excuse for a speech.

Mika knew she'd take him back tomorrow—she tended to be forgiving when it came to men with a billion dollars at their disposal—but for tonight he could drink cheap swill with the rest of the riff-raff.

The person to fill the open spot was the evening's Master of Ceremonies. The Southern Gentleman was not only somewhat of a celebrity, but he'd also worked his way into the social circles Mika cared about most—the rich and famous.

"Care to join a few of us in the lounge afterward?" she'd casually asked the man who billed himself as The Southern Gentleman.

"It would be my great honor, ma'am," he drawled.

With all eighteen of the chosen gathered around her in the lounge, Mika looked at her watch and led the countdown: "Five... four... three... two... one... zero. Black Midnight has officially begun!" With great fanfare, the cognac was poured, and the cigars cut and lit.

Mika looked up and saw an uninvited guest walking in her direction.

Dane.

"Invitation only, Dane," Mika said sharply.

"Don't worry, I'm not staying," Dane replied. "I just wanted to know if you'd seen Koda. He never came to the room. I've looked everywhere, and he's nowhere to be found."

"How would I know?" Mika asked. "Now, if you don't mind..."

"Excuse me," the Southern Gentleman drawled, "but it seems Mr. Mulvaney is comin' through the lobby door as we speak. And if you don't mind me sayin', it looks like your friend has just seen a ghost."

LAKE PONCHARTRAIN, LOUISIANA
SEPTEMBER 21, 1927

There were three events that made 1927 a memorable year for Onyx Webb.

The first event was the Great Flood, a disaster that decimated the bayou and surrounding area for hundreds of miles, setting in motion a mass exodus—including many of Onyx's friends and neighbors—cutting the region's population in half.

The second thing was an explosion of artistic creativity that possessed Onyx with a constant need to express herself— writing, drawing, painting, poetry, photography, singing—and any other art form imaginable. It was exactly what Onyx's mother, Jofranka, said would happen.

"Onyx is half-ghost, Andre, the child of a human and a ghost," Jofranka had told Catfish. *"When the time comes, her need for energy will be insatiable—you must help her feed that need every way you can, for creative energy is the source of life."*

Catfish Webb did not want his daughter to be a *half-ghost*, whatever that would entail. He wanted Onyx to be 100 percent human—100 percent alive—like him.

Though he'd been warned, Catfish found himself in an ongoing state of denial, as if ignoring the truth would not make it so. So, when—at the age of twenty-nine—Onyx began begging Catfish to buy her pencils, paper, and other art supplies, he balked at the requests.

"A young woman needs to be out of doors," Catfish told her, "in nature, child, not cooped up inside."

"That's the thing, Papa! I want to draw trees and deer and streams and rocks and birds and glorious sunsets!" Onyx exclaimed, twirling in circles in the old houseboat. "I want to capture every beautiful thing in all its majestic glory, Daddy, please please please please please!"

Catfish continued to avoid his daughter's requests until one day she began ranting about wanting a piano.

"Fine, fine," Catfish said. "I will get you some paints and a drawing canvas or two, but there'll be no piano. A heavy thing like that could fall right through the floor into the swamp."

* * *

There was something else that happened in 1927 that would have a profound impact on Onyx...

She met Ulrich.

Onyx was sitting on a stool with a canvas and her paints, directly across from the Tchefuncte River lighthouse on the northern shore of Lake Ponchartrain, when she saw him. Even from forty yards away she could tell the man was handsome, his bronzed muscles gleaming in the southern sun.

He was also suspended a hundred feet in the air from a rope tethered to the railing atop the lighthouse, a bucket of whitewash hanging by his side. The irony that they were painting the lighthouse at the same time—even if painting it in different ways—was not lost on her.

"I've blossomed into a woman of marrying age, Daddy!" Onyx had declared to her father years earlier. *"It's time for me to find a man, bear children, go places, and have a life of my own."*

Every time Onyx broached the subject, Catfish simply put her off.

"What's the rush, child? The right one'll come along, and when he does, you'll know. The right one just ain't appeared yet is all."

Onyx felt she'd waited long enough.

This was the one.

She just knew it.

Onyx continued painting, carefully applying the final few brushstrokes to her canvas and trying not to think about the man—as if that were possible—while the August sun beat down hard on her.

Eventually, the man climbed down off the lighthouse and made his way toward her. She worked hard to pretend she hadn't seen him coming, continuing to paint until she was suddenly covered in shade.

Onyx looked up at the large, muscled man standing over her. "What are you painting?" he asked in a strong German accent, pronouncing the word *what* as *vhat*.

"I am painting you," Onyx said.

"Me? Might I see your masterpiece?" the German asked as he stepped behind Onyx without waiting for her to answer.

Onyx waited in suspense for his response.

"It is nice but boring," the German said, noticing a look of disappointment spreading on Onyx's face. "Not the painting," the German added quickly. "I mean the lighthouse is boring. The painting is marvelous, but the lighthouse is all white—no color, no pattern, nothing to draw the eye to a focal point."

Onyx exhaled, realizing she had been holding her breath in anticipation of his response.

"I guess you are right," Onyx said, her cheeks blushing.

"There is no guessing about it!" the German declared. "My father was a collector of fine art and taught me of such things."

The handsome German extended his hand. "My name is Ulrich, Ulrich Schröder."

"Onyx Webb," Onyx said, taking Ulrich's weather-worn hand in hers and shaking it.

"Well, Miss Webb, perhaps when you return tomorrow to finish your painting, the lighthouse will not be so boring."

"But what if my painting is already complete, Mr. Schröder?" Onyx said playing along, having gained confidence by sensing his interest in her.

"That would be a tragedy for us both," Ulrich said. "When fate draws two people together, it is the job of man to comply."

Fate, thought Onyx.

Yes, it was fate.

*   *   *

The following day, when Onyx returned to the shore of Lake Ponchartrain, she saw that a two-foot-wide black stripe had been painted down the center of the lighthouse. Minutes later, as Onyx was setting up her easel, Ulrich approached carrying a basket of freshly made Natchitoches pies, cornbread, jellied preserves, and a bottle of wine.

"You see?" Ulrich said, spreading a blanket on the ground. "Your painting *was* incomplete."

Other than her father, no man had ever lavished Onyx with such attention in all her twenty-nine years on Earth.

"If you are trying to get my attention, Ulrich Schröder," Onyx said, her cheeks once again in full blush, "please know that you have succeeded."

SAVANNAH, GEORGIA
JUNE 3, 1979

Wyatt Scrogger was still hung over.

He'd been sound asleep when he thought he heard someone pounding on the door to his apartment. So he did what any self-respecting college student would do. He wrapped his pillow around his head and ignored it.

At least he tried to, but whoever it was continued pounding and then started calling his name. "Wyatt Scrogger, open up. Police."

The last part got his attention.

4:42 p.m.

Wyatt answered Detective Leo Igler's questions as fully and as honestly as was possible under the conditions, more accurately, *his* condition.

"So you say you arrived at Pinkie Masters about 8:15 p.m., had a few beers and then moved to where?" Leo asked.

"Like I said, I had a few too many to remember where I went," Scrogger said. "I was celebrating the end of my junior year at South University of Pharmacy."

"I thought you said you wanted to be a comedian?" Leo said.

"Yeah, well, my Dad's a pharmacist and he figures that when I fail it will be good to have something to fall back on," Scrogger said. "Before we go any further, could you please tell me what I'm doing here?"

"We'll get to that," Leo said. "Now, just so I've got this straight, you stopped by a friend's house around 7:30, went home and had dinner, headed over to Pinkie's on foot between 8:00 and 8:15, and after that you have no explanation for where you were or who you were with, correct?"

"Have you ever had a few too many beers, detective?" Scrogger asked. "What happens is that things get blurry and then hazy and then—wait, I think there's a technical term for it—oh, yeah, it's called being drunk. Am I being arrested for having gotten drunk last night and killing some brain cells?"

"Tell me about your answering machine," Leo said.

"My answering machine?"

Leo remained silent, waited.

"I think it's a Phone Mate Model 400-S," Scrogger said, his mind beginning to race, his wheels turning, trying to figure out why the detective would ask about that.

"Oh, yeah, I forgot you were studying to become a comedian," Leo said. "How about you tell me some of your funniest answering machine lines?"

"Okay," Scrogger said. "Hello, you've reached the Scrogg. You have the right to remain silent, but if you do, it's going to be hard to return your call."

"That's pretty good, kid" Leo said. "You got any more?"

"More? I got a million of them," Scrogger said with a certain amount of pride. "Hello, this is Death. I am not in right now, but if you leave your name and number, I'll be right with you. Twinkle, twinkle, little star, bet you're wondering..."

"How about drugging girls," Leo said, interrupting Scrogger. "You know, so you can abduct them and maybe have sex with them? You got anything like that?" Leo asked.

Scrogger went silent. "What is this about?"

Leo reached into his desk and produced a tape recorder and set it on the middle of his desk. He placed his index finger on the play button and paused for dramatic effect.

"Before we came out to roust you from your nap, we tried to reach you by phone. Of course, you didn't answer, but your machine did. I found the message to be very interesting, so I called back and taped it. But to be honest, kid, I didn't think it was very funny under the circumstances."

"The circumstances?" Scrogger asked. "What...?"

"When was the last time you say you saw Juniper Cole, Mr. Scrogger?"

"Juniper? I told you I stopped by her house, I mean Quinn's house, last night. About 7:30, what in the hell is this about?"

"And you claim you didn't see Miss Cole after that?" Leo asked.

"No, I mean yes, I didn't see Juniper after that," Scrogger said. "Did something happen to Juniper?"

Leo lowered his index finger and pushed the recorder's play button. *"Hey, you've reached the Scrogg. I'm probably in a bar trying to get a girl to sleep with me. But as the saying goes: Roses impress, liquor works fine, but if in a rush, use ketamine."*

Beep.

ORLANDO, FLORIDA
JANUARY 25, 2010

t had been two days since the Restoring Savannah banquet, and the girl in the mirror was all Koda could talk about.

"Think what you want, Dane, but I saw her," Koda said for the third time, getting up from the leather sofa in the apartment in the 55 West building and starting to pace.

"You gotta get a grip, man," Dane said. "Mika is still fuming about your speech, and I don't want to be around when word gets back to your dad."

"I saw her, Dane."

"How many vodkas did you have?" Dane asked. "Five?"

"I... saw... her," Koda said again.

"Okay, okay. You saw a girl in a mirror," Dane said. "But I don't get why you're so freaked out?"

"We're best friends, right, Dane?" Koda asked.

"You gotta ask?" Dane was tempted to mention the fact that Koda had punched him in the face when they were at the bar at the Forsyth Park Hotel, but didn't.

"And in the four years you've known me, have I ever lied to you?" Koda asked. "About anything?"

Dane shook his head. Like most people, Koda Mulvaney had character flaws, but being a liar was not among them.

"Then listen to what I'm saying, okay?" Koda said. "I'm not telling you I saw a girl's reflection in a mirror—*I'm telling you I saw a girl in a mirror. She was in... the... glass.*"

Dane went silent and took in what he'd just been told. "Okay, what color was her hair?

"Gray."

"So it was an old woman," Dane said.

"No," Koda said, shaking his head. "She was young, like late teens or early twenties maybe."

"With gray hair?"

"Not just her hair," Koda said. "Her face, her clothes, everything. It was *all* gray."

"A gray girl in a gray place with gray clothing," Dane repeated, trying to make sense of it. "What was she wearing?"

"I'm not sure," Koda said. "Wait." Koda closed his eyes, tried to summon a mental image in his mind. "A dress. No, not a dress. A fancy gown, like someone would wear to a wedding."

"Weren't there a couple of weddings...?"

"Don't go there," Koda said.

"Okay, okay," Dane said. "Did she say anything?"

Koda shook his head from side to side.

"Was she pretty?" Dane asked.

"Oh, yeah," Koda said. "But there was something else..."

"What?"

"It's hard to explain, to put into words," Koda said, closing his eyes again, trying to form a picture of the girl in his mind. "It was her eyes. There was something in her eyes—a combination of innocence and confusion—like she was..."

"Lost?" Dane asked.

"No, not lost," Koda said. "Like she was dead."

*   *   *

That night Dane took a shower and headed over to DJ's Chophouse down the block on Church Street, hoping the pretty brunette bartender he'd met a few weeks earlier—Robyn—happened to be working.

Koda stayed home in bed, tossing and turning, thinking about a girl too. *The girl in the mirror.*

LAKE PONCHARTRAIN, LOUISIANA
DECEMBER 30, 1927

"Tell me why, Daddy?" Onyx demanded, tears streaming down her face. "Ulrich is a good man, and I love him—and he loves me."

"Because I am your father, and I forbid it!" Catfish said.

"Say it, Daddy," Onyx said.

"Say what?"

"It's because he's German," Onyx said.

"That's not the reason, Jitterbug," Catfish said. "Besides, you hardly know the man."

"You only knew Mama for a week, Daddy," Onyx said. "There's only one other thing it can be. You want to keep me to yourself. To replace Mama. Well, I won't let you steal my life from me. I am twenty-nine years of age. I want to travel, I want to paint, I want to have children—I refuse to die a spinster doing laundry for her daddy in the swamp!" Onyx said, then stormed from the houseboat.

In that moment, Catfish knew he could no longer postpone the inevitable; it was time to do what he should have done years earlier. He must do what he'd promised Jofranka so long ago, in this very room. He must tell Onyx everything.

Then she'll understand.

Catfish walked to the door and called out after her: "Tomorrow, Jitterbug, on your birthday. We talk about it then."

Onyx kept walking.

* * *

In three decades with his daughter, the only things Onyx had ever begged her father for were art supplies, a piano, and to marry Ulrich.

Art supplies were easy.

Giving his blessing to marry Ulrich was out of the question.

A piano would have to suffice.

It took three large men to transport the Blasius & Sons grand piano—which Catfish had ordered by sending a cable to the company in Philadelphia six weeks earlier—from the train platform forty-six miles away to the houseboat.

Blasius & Sons were known for exceptional craftsmanship and celebrity endorsements, including that of Thomas Edison, who'd used a Blasius & Sons grand for his experiments with phonograph recordings. Or so the company's newspaper advertisements claimed.

Making things especially difficult was getting the monstrous piano onto the houseboat in the dark of night, without so much as a grunt or a groan. He wanted to avoid waking Onyx, making the piano a surprise gift when she awoke on the morning of her thirtieth birthday.

Once the men left, Catfish made the rest of the preparations: writing out her card, putting candles on the cake, and decorating the entire place with red and purple crepe paper streamers.

There was only one more thing to do.

Catfish pried up several floorboards to expose a hidden compartment that held only one thing—Jofranka's red leather keepsake box. It had been his wife's dying wish that he give the box to Onyx when the appropriate time had arrived.

It finally had.

Besides the clothes on her back, the red keepsake box was the only thing Jofranka carried out of the woods with her after they'd gotten married.

Catfish once asked Jofranka what was in the box.

"Secrets," was all his wife would say.

Catfish never asked about the contents of the box again, nor did he ever look inside. It belonged to Onyx, not him.

He placed the box on the piano next to the cake and birthday card, then tried to get some sleep.

* * *

Onyx was usually an early riser, so Catfish was surprised when the clock struck nine the following morning, and she'd yet to come out of her room. He made his way down the hall and rapped on her door.

Onyx didn't answer.

Catfish knocked again, still no response.

Catfish opened the door and looked in. He could see Onyx lying motionless beneath the covers. "Jitterbug?" Catfish said.

She did not respond.

She did not move.

Catfish's heart began to race, something was wrong. He made his way to the side of the bed and pulled back the covers.

Onyx wasn't in the bed, just three large feather pillows.

A quick look around the room confirmed Catfish's worst fears—her clothing, photo albums, and other important belongings, as well as her suitcase—were gone.

Oh, sweet child, what have you done?

SAVANNAH, GEORGIA
JUNE 3, 1979

Juniper had been awake for almost an hour, the drug she'd been given finally wearing off. She tried to move her arms, but they were strapped to a metal table.

So were her legs.

Though she was covered by a thin blanket, she could tell her clothes had been removed.

She heard the sound of footsteps and moments later the door swung open. When the man entered the room, Juniper immediately noticed three things.

First, the man was no longer in a wheelchair as he had been when she encountered him near the fountain in Forsyth Park.

Second, he wasn't overweight.

Third, he seemed younger than the night before. It had all been a disguise. *How could she have been so naive?*

"What's your middle name?" he asked.

"Who are you really?" Juniper asked. "Are you even with the police?"

"When I ask you a question, I expect an answer," he said. "What is your middle name?"

"Why do you want to know?" Juniper replied.

The man released a long breath. "Because I'd like to do some anagrams of your name. It's a game where you mix up letters to spell other things. Please don't make me ask again."

Juniper fought the urge to scream or cry or pull on her restraints, knowing it was probably what he wanted. "Is that what this is to you? A game?"

"Tell me your middle name, Juniper, and I promise things will be okay," he said, knowing the statement was a lie.

Juniper knew it was a lie, too. Quinn had been right all along. There were evil people in the world, and you could never be too safe because you never really knew who you could trust.

"How do you know my name?" Juniper asked.

"I've been watching TV. I know everything about you. It seems you're quite the celebrity. Juniper this, Juniper that. Maybe I'll bring the TV down for you later, but first, tell me your God damn middle name."

There was an edge to his voice now.

"Are you promising to let me go?" Juniper asked.

"I can promise things will go better," he said.

Juniper didn't want to find out what might happen if she pushed him too hard. "Ann," she said finally.

"With an 'e' on the end or without?"

"Without," Juniper said.

There was a long silence, then he said: "My mother's middle name was Ann. She was a saint who smelled like vanilla and loved me very much."

"You're lucky," Juniper said, trying to make a connection with him. "My mother usually smells like gin and..."

"Did I ask about your mother?" the man snapped.

"No, but—"

The man leaned in close to Juniper, his face just inches from hers. Juniper froze. Strapped to the metal table as she was, there was nowhere she could go.

"Did I ask about your mother?"

Juniper shook her head from side to side, doing her best to fight back the fear and the tears that she knew would eventually come.

And now they did, a river of uncontrollable tears.

He leaned back. "Don't," he said. "Don't cry. I used to cry when I wanted things to be different, and it never helped. Crying never solved a thing."

*   *   *

Sergent Elton Nahum sat at the kitchen table finishing his lunch—a tuna fish sandwich with sliced pickles on white bread with the crust trimmed off, just as his mother used to make—waiting for the local news to start.

At the center of the table was a plastic cup filled with wooden Scrabble® letters. Nahum dumped the letters on the table and searched through them until he found the ones he needed:

J-U-N-I-P-E-R A-N-N C-O-L-E

Then Nahum began rearranging the letters to see what other combinations he could create...

Penn Lace Junior...

Sounded like a boy's name, so he rearranged the letters again:

Jenna Nicole Pru...

He was pretty sure "Pru" wasn't a word.

Juno Linn Pearce.

Better.

Can Opener In Jul.

The last one was pretty good, and he smiled. He moved the letters around again and the smile quickly faded:

Rape Junno Cline.

Nahum did not like rape. To his mind, rape was wrong, a barbaric act of violence carried out by someone who'd never found a more creative way of coping with their anger.

Nahum downed the last of his A&W root beer just as WTOC-TV reporter Skylar Savage appeared on the TV screen.

"Wyatt Allen Scrogger—who police say has been questioned once but remains only a person of interest—was brought in by the Savannah PD for additional questioning," the blonde reporter said with significant drama, her hair flapping in the warm afternoon breeze.

Skylar Savage. Nahum loathed the sight of her, with that enormous fake smile, a mouth filled with too many teeth, and her red lips that she undoubtedly painted on throughout the day.

Who in the hell names their child Skylar, anyway? It sounded more like a car model than a girl's name. Skylar probably wasn't the reporter's real name—just something the bimbo concocted as part of her quest to land an anchor position in a major market, like New York or Chicago, or perhaps Atlanta. Savannah was, after all, just a small-time, minor-league market at best.

"Yes, Skylar, that's right," co-anchor Domingo Gutierrez replied from the studio, "but my sources at the Savannah PD say he's been released, and still no charges have been filed."

Then Quinn Cole came on the screen and made a plea for information on his missing sister as throngs of volunteers searched one of the city's many squares behind him.

As pathetic as the girl's brother looked on the TV, crying and begging, he was right. Juniper Cole was special.

Nahum never met anyone like her before.

She had a vibrancy in her that was hard to describe, as if someone had taken pure light and filled her soul with it.

In that way, she was his polar opposite.

Inside, he was nothing but darkness.

Nahum grabbed his fake-belly pillow and shoved it up under his shirt. It was time to get back to his job at the Savannah P.D.

SAVANNAH, GEORGIA
JANUARY 30, 2010

The manager of the Forsyth Park Hotel was waiting in the lobby when they arrived.

"Good morning, Mr. Mulvaney, Mr. Luckner," he said in a tone that made it clear he did not appreciate the scene the young men had made a week earlier in the hotel lobby bar. "You wish to discuss something of an urgent nature?"

"I want to buy one of your mirrors," Koda said. Four consecutive sleepless nights had driven Koda to the point where he could think of no other option.

"One of our mirrors?" the hotel manager asked. "I don't understand."

"I'm not in the position to explain," Koda continued, pulling out his checkbook and pen. "I would appreciate it if you could just give me the price, so I can write you a check and get on my way."

"Hotel property is not for sale," the hotel manager said.

"Of course, it is," Koda said. "Everything is for sale."

The hotel manager stayed silent.

"I've had a rough week, and I'm in no mood for haggling," Koda said. "Just tell me the price."

"Which mirror?"

"In the hallway upstairs, near the piano lounge," Koda said.

"That mirror is a one-of-a-kind piece," the hotel manager said. "I would think the price would be nothing short of $10,000, assuming the hotel..."

"Is that your best price?" Koda asked.

"It's my only price," the hotel manager said.

Koda pulled out his cell phone, pressed a button and waited. "Hey, Mika. Listen, I'm here at the Forsyth to buy the mirror you wanted and the hotel manager says ten grand is the best he can do. Uh huh, uh huh, I'll ask..."

The hotel manager went gray.

"Ms. Flagler wants to know if..."

"Please tell Ms. Flagler I had no idea the mirror was for her," the hotel manager said. "I'm sure we can go down to $5,000."

"He's telling me $5,000 now," Koda said into the phone, then made a face. "Uh huh, uh huh..."

A look of realization—or perhaps it was a look of fear—flashed across the manager's face. "Tell Ms. Flagler we'd be thrilled to offer the mirror as a gift for her years of patronage," the hotel manager said. "Please ask her where she'd like it delivered."

"He says the hotel is gifting it to you," Koda said into the phone. "Which house do you want it delivered to? Uh huh, uh huh, okay, will do—I love you too, sugar-lumps. Bye."

Koda clicked off. "Mika says I should just take it with me."

"You and Mika sounded pretty lovey-dovey," Dane said once they were outside. "I didn't even know you two were talking after the speech thing."

"We aren't," Koda said. "I was talking to my voicemail."

CHICAGO, ILLINOIS
OCTOBER 28, 1929

The Roaring Twenties were a time of massive wealth and extreme excess. Unfortunately, none of that wealth or excess seemed to make its way to Onyx and Ulrich.

The problems between them started the very first night after Onyx had packed her things and snuck away in the middle of the night two years earlier. When they boarded the train in New Orleans, bound for Chicago, Ulrich suggested they spend a few extra dollars and get a sleeper car.

"Who wants to sit out here with the rabble when we can travel in luxury?" Ulrich asked. But when Ulrich pulled off his shirt and started to undo the buckle on his belt, Onyx realized his true motive was not luxury but, rather, of a carnal nature.

"Ulrich, what are you doing?" Onyx asked.

Ulrich shot Onyx a quizzical look. "We can't be very good together in the bed with our clothes on, can we?"

"Listen, Ulrich, I do love you but—"

"Yes, you love me. And I love you," Ulrich said, reaching a hand toward Onyx's breast, which she quickly slapped away.

"You wish to sleep with me, Ulrich? These are my terms," Onyx said, much to Ulrich's amusement. "We will lie together once we are husband and wife, not a minute before."

"Are you finished?" Ulrich asked.

"No," Onyx said. "I will also not marry a man who is not gainfully employed. So, Ulrich Schröder, I suggest you look for a job the minute we get off the train, and then make your proposal. Until that time, enjoy the luxury of your sleeping car." Onyx closed the door behind her, leaving the half-dressed German to ponder what had just happened.

Ulrich apparently got the message. Four days after their arrival, he had secured a job installing windows at the Steven's Hotel on Chicago's lakeshore. The largest and most expensive hotel in the world—with almost 3,000 rooms—The Stevens had become the epicenter of the exciting, bustling metropolis.

With his job papers in hand, Ulrich immediately asked Onyx for her hand. Two days later—January 6, 1928—they were married by a justice of the peace.

But now, twenty-one months later—on what should have been one of the best days of her life—Onyx found herself sitting on the edge of the bed in a small downtown Chicago hotel room, waiting for Ulrich to finally turn up. It was times like these that Onyx questioned why she'd run off with the man.

For almost two years, Onyx had socked away every dollar she made waiting tables at the Oak Room, dancing as part of a stage show review at Chicago's Chez Paree nightclub—along with whatever meager amount she could siphon from Ulrich's weekly paycheck—she was able to cobble enough for the down payment on their first home. It was a single-level bungalow in the 6200 block of W. Byron Street, not far from Mt. Olive Cemetery and the Dunning Asylum. She would finally have a home.

The mistake Onyx made was asking Ulrich to get the cashier's check for $900 from the bank and bring it with him to the closing.

Ulrich never arrived.

*   *   *

At one o'clock in the morning the door to the room swung open, and Ulrich came in carrying roses and singing loudly...

> *"Blue skies, smilin' at me,*
> *Nothin' but blue skies do I see..."*

Onyx sat up in bed. "You're drunk."

It was the Prohibition era, with laws making alcohol consumption illegal sweeping the country, but that didn't mean there weren't ways to get a drink if one was so inclined. Onyx learned early that Ulrich was *so inclined* virtually every day of the week.

"Yes, drunk with possibilities." Ulrich said, tossing the flowers on the bed. "Today I met a man…"

"You missed the closing, Ulrich," Onyx said, forcing down the anger that was beginning to rise in her throat.

"Yes, yes," Ulrich slurred. "But I am trying to tell you, Onyx, I met a man…"

"In a pig bar, no doubt," Onyx said.

Though Onyx had never visited one of the hundreds of illegal watering holes scattered throughout the city of Chicago, she knew there were two types of bars.

The first was the speakeasy, which catered to the upper-crust of society, with passwords that changed daily required for entry.

The second type of establishment was the pig bar. These were low-class places that exploited a loop-hole in the law forbidding the sale of alcoholic beverages by charging twenty-five cents to glimpse an attraction—such as a pig—and then providing the customer with a gratuitous shot of gin, thus circumventing the law.

"Yes, he was in a bar, so what?" Ulrich said. "He's a very important business man…"

"An important man?" Onyx said. "An important man who you met in a pig bar? Listen to yourself, Ulrich."

"He works for the Chicago Stock Exchange, Onyx, and he told me of a once in a lifetime opportunity, so I invested…"

Onyx lowered her head and began to cry; there was no need to hear the rest of the story. "Get it back, Ulrich. First thing in the morning, you go to this man…"

"Damn it, Onyx!" Ulrich shouted. "I am the man of this family! You think Mr. Rockefeller and Mr. Carnegie made their fortunes playing it safe? I am telling you, the stocks he told me of will make us millions. Then I will buy you all the houses you want, more houses than we can even live in!"

Onyx turned out the light and lay back down. "Get the money back, Ulrich," her voice came from the dark. "Just get it back."

* * *

The next day—October 29, 1929—Ulrich worked his eight hours installing windows from scaffolding hanging on the outside of the eleventh floor of the hotel. Besides an unusual amount of noise from police sirens on the streets below, it was an uneventful day.

When his shift ended, Ulrich went to the Purple Pig in the 4800 block of N. Broadway, the establishment he'd been at the day before—its attraction being a Greenland pig covered in purple paint, thus the name. But the man from the stock market was nowhere to be seen.

"Get me a gin," Ulrich said to the bartender. "On second thought, make it a double."

"Everyone's drinking doubles today," the bartender said, reaching back and briefly lifting the blanket to expose the sleeping pig for less than a second, then went to work pouring Ulrich's drink. "Bad news is always good news for a bar. It drives people to drink."

Ulrich froze, the bartender's words finally settling in.

"The bad news?"

"Yeah, you know, the stock market crash," the bartender said, setting Ulrich's double gin on the bar in front of him. "Lost 11 percent at the opening bell, the market did, and it only got worse from there. What, you didn't hear?"

"You mean the stock market—it, it..."

"Thirty billion dollars up in smoke. Can you imagine?" the bartender asked. "They're calling it Black Friday."

Ulrich grabbed the glass and downed the double gin in one gulp. "The man who was here yesterday? The one in the nice suit with the carnation on his lapel?"

The bartender shook his head. "Shame, huh? Can you imagine jumping from the top of a building?" the bartender asked. "I mean, over money?"

Yes, Ulrich thought.

Yes, I can.

* * *

It only took a day before all construction on the hotel was halted—temporarily everyone was told.

How temporary was temporary?

No one knew.

The day after that, Onyx's shifts at the restaurant were cut back to almost nothing. Buying a house now—even if they had the money—was out of the question. They couldn't even pay the rent on their room.

Three days after that, Ulrich and Onyx were on a train to New York City, where Ulrich said he could get a job with his brother, Lucas.

"My brother owns the biggest art gallery in all of New York," Ulrich said. "The Schröder Gallery in Times Square. I'm told it is right in the middle of everything," Ulrich said.

"Told?" Onyx asked. "You've not been there?"

"Well, no," Ulrich said.

"It will take the last of our funds just to get there," Onyx said. "Are you sure he will hire you?" Onyx asked.

"Of course," Ulrich said. "He must. He's my brother."

SAVANNAH, GEORGIA
JUNE 4, 1979

onsidered by many to be one of the most beautiful cities in America, Savannah was the oldest city in Georgia and a case study in excellent urban planning. Originally designed as a place for colonists to conduct military exercises, the city was laid out in a distinct grid pattern of streets and squares. As such, it took less than an hour for authorities to organize a grid search for Juniper Cole.

Forsyth Park was established as the LPS (Last Point Seen) and served as one of two command locations, the second being the obelisk in the center of Johnson Square.

By its very nature, a grid search tended to move in a slow and methodical way, with volunteers sent out to find clues and report back.

Six hours in, no clues had been discovered. No one had seen a thing.

Quinn Cole was beside himself.

Helicopters flew overhead at night, lights shining down in fields and backyards.

Nothing.

Twelve hours into the search, leaders began to ask questions. Should they expand the search area? How far beyond the LPS should they go? Maybe it was just a bastard search, one in which the person wasn't really lost at all. People were tired and tensions were running high. Maybe the girl is just "shacked up" with her boyfriend somewhere.

Quinn did interview after interview, showing Juniper's picture and asking anyone who'd seen her to come forward.

No one had.

The hours wore on, but nothing changed.

In Loll...

The girl stumbled forward through the grayness, the faint echo of thunder in the distance.

She tilted her head back and gazed upward, lifting her eyes to a sky that was neither light nor dark, neither day nor night. It simply ... was.

How long had she been here, wherever this was? How long had she been walking? It couldn't have been too long. Her legs were not tired.

She looked down, trained her eyes on her legs and watched them in amazement as they did their job, moving her forward with grace and efficiency.

I have legs, she thought.

Then she remembered the boy; the dark-haired young man with the scar on his forehead looking back at her. Where was that? Oh, yes, the hotel.

She'd been there many times before, she knew.

That's when the mirror had caught her eye.

She'd seen the mirror before but had always followed the rules.

There were three unbreakable rules:

Rule one: Do not touch an animal.

Rule two: Do not touch another person.

Rule three: Never, ever, under any circumstance, touch a mirror.

Where had the rules come from? She did not know. She just knew them.

Everyone did.

But then—as if she knew there was something beyond where she was; another world, another life—she reached out and touched the mirror.

And she was right.

She made her way to the old building, up the stairs and past the piano, then down the hallway.

She knew why she'd come back to this place.

She was going to break the rule again.

She was going to touch the mirror.

Damn the rules.

Would the boy still be there?

But when she got to the end of the hallway, the mirror was gone.

NEW YORK CITY
JUNE 23, 1931

Much of the last two and a half years in New York had been financial hell.

Onyx and Ulrich arrived from Chicago virtually broke, used the last of their savings for a small apartment in a rat-infested building in Brooklyn, and scraped by as best they could. Meals were often at free soup kitchens crowded with scores of other victims of the "Great Depression."

Ulrich told Onyx he could get work with his brother, Lucas, but he had been wrong. When he approached his brother, Lucas told Ulrich that when Ulrich abandoned the family business, he'd abandoned the family as well. "As far as the Schröder family is concerned," Lucas said, "you are dead to us all."

"Maybe Lucas will change his mind?" Onyx asked.

"I told you to never speak of my brother in this house!" Ulrich shouted. "Lucas is a back-stabbing rat!"

With no work to be had, Ulrich crawled even deeper into the bottle, so much so that Onyx had come to believe her husband was a certified alcoholic. But, ironically, Ulrich's drinking led to a chance meeting with a guy in a bar—a Mohawk Indian, of all people—who helped Ulrich get an exciting but extremely dangerous job working construction on the Empire State building.

"Another construction job?" Onyx asked.

"It's because of what I did for a living before coming to the United States," Ulrich said. It was the first time her husband had shared anything about his life before they met. Every time Onyx had asked about his past he refused to talk about it.

"What did you do?" Onyx asked.

"I was a trapeze artist," Ulrich said.

"You were a trapeze artist?" Onyx said, breaking into laughter.

Ulrich nodded, his face serious.

"You're serious," Onyx said.

"My father and mother started the show, with all of their children expected to become part of the troupe," Ulrich said. "The six of us—my parents, Lucas, and my younger brother and sister, Jan and Lisileto—we were the Soaring Schröders of Berlin."

Onyx remained silent for a few seconds, but then could not contain herself, bursting into laughter again.

"This is why I don't speak of it!" Ulrich said storming out of the room and slamming the door behind him.

At least now Onyx understood why every time her husband did find work it was always dangling on the outside of a building at the end of a rope.

* * *

Ulrich had not taken his brother's rejection well and forbade Onyx from having any contact with Lucas, but fate had other plans.

To make ends meet, Onyx decided to try to sell her artwork. She had been painting on and off their entire time together, whenever funds would allow.

Within months, Onyx was out-earning her husband, though it wasn't hard to do. While some men would have been threatened by their wives' success, it gave Ulrich more cash to go drinking with the boys.

Initially, Onyx tried selling her art from street corners, but with times being tough for so many people, she had few buyers. Knowing the major galleries only dealt with established artists, she needed to find another way to get her work seen by people with wealth.

Onyx was walking down the street, a completed canvas under her arm, when she saw a well-dressed man holding the door open for an equally well-dressed woman.

It was the door to a restaurant.

Within months, Onyx had placed her art—on a consignment basis—in six upscale eateries in Manhattan. It was the perfect quid pro quo; they were delighted to sell her work for a share of the proceeds, and she desperately needed the money.

The biggest challenge facing Onyx was transporting her finished paintings on busses and trains from their small apartment in Brooklyn into the city. Selling her work anywhere else was futile. She needed to display her work where people with money lived and worked.

Manhattan was the only answer.

"I've found a better place for us to live," Onyx told Ulrich one day. Ulrich was laying on the sofa, reading a three-day old copy of the *New York Times* he'd dug out of a corner trash bin.

"What's wrong with living here?" Ulrich asked, not bothering to look up at her.

"I need to be near my customers," Onyx said. "I've found a place on West Forty-Sixth Street, just around the corner from Times Square."

"West Forty-Sixth?" Ulrich replied. "How much do they want for this place?"

"They wanted $125 per month, but they agreed to $95," Onyx said.

"Agreed? What are you saying?"

"I'm saying I'm tired of sharing a bath and having no place to store my work," Onyx said. "I've signed a lease and—"

"Signed a lease? Did I say you could—?"

"Please don't argue with me, Ulrich," Onyx said. "We move in at the end of the month."

"But..."

"It is done, Ulrich," Onyx said.

*   *   *

One day, as fate would have it, Lucas Schröder was dining with a friend at the 21 Club on West Fifty-Second Street, a place where the table you were given said a lot about who you were. He'd just placed his order for steak tartar when he spotted one of Onyx's pieces on the wall.

"That painting, who is the artist?" Lucas asked.

"Onyx," the maître'd said.

"Does this Onyx have a last name?" Lucas asked.

The maître'd shrugged. "She comes in on Tuesday to drop off new paintings and collect for anything we've sold, that's all I know."

A week later, Lucas Schröder sat in the 21 Club bar waiting for the mysterious artist, Onyx, to arrive. When she did, Lucas handed Onyx his business card and told her he wanted to sell her work in his gallery.

Onyx looked at the card. "I can't," she said handing the card back to him.

Lucas dealt with artists every day, most of them begging to have their work placed in his gallery.

"I don't think you realize who I am," Lucas said.

"I don't think you realize who I am," Onyx replied. "I am your sister-in-law, Onyx Schröder. I am Ulrich's wife."

*   *   *

Intrigued with the woman, Lucas insisted they talk and Onyx reluctantly agreed. Lucas revealed that Ulrich had said nothing about having a wife.

"Would it have made a difference?" Onyx said.

"Not in the slightest," Lucas told her. "Ulrich is a drunken scoundrel with no work ethic." Onyx agreed, having found out the hard way. Then the conversation turned to what had brought them together in the first place.

Art.

When Onyx finally glanced at her watch, she was shocked to see how quickly four hours could go by when talking with the right man about some shared interest.

Unfortunately for Lucas, no matter how many times he asked Onyx to relent, she would not agree to place her art in his gallery. "Ulrich has forbidden me to talk with you, so even this was a breach of my word." That's when Lucas came up with the idea for Onyx to study with Hans Hoffman.

"You know Hans Hoffman?" Onyx asked.

"Know him? His work hangs in my gallery," Lucas said.

"Under one condition," Onyx said. "Neither of us may tell Ulrich of this arrangement."

"That, and Hoffman agrees to accept you. I have yet to even show him your work."

SAVANNAH, GEORGIA
JUNE 4, 1979

No one would believe that pretending to be a paraplegic could be so exhausting, Sergent Elton Nahum thought to himself.

But it was.

Yes, getting to sit all day was a plus, but rolling around in the chair using nothing but his arms was more exhausting than walking, by a long shot. Combine that with having been up most of the night before watching the TV news coverage on the disappearance of local mini-celebrity Juniper Cole, and he was exhausted.

He'd been lying in bed the night before, watching that blonde-bubble head, Skylar Savage, again— Juniper Cole's light blue prom dress hanging on the back of the door, her shoes and yellow panties in a plastic bag sitting on the floor beneath it— when the idea had hit him.

Nahum sat up in bed, opened the nightstand drawer and pulled out a box containing more Scrabble® letters, something he kept in every part of the house. He found the letters he needed:

S-E-R-G-E-N-T E-L-T-O-N N-A-H-U-M

Then, as he'd done earlier—Nahum began rearranging them until he'd found a name he liked:

G-L-E-N-N-A T-H-O-M-S-E-N - T-R-U-E

How ironic, Nahum thought. He was a man... pretending to be a woman... telling an enormous lie... with the last name *True*.

Hilarious.

And he'd finally get to use the voice modulator he'd purchased a year earlier.

Now, sitting at his desk across from Leo Igler—watching the old detective toil away, trying to decide if he should arrest Wyatt Scrogger for Juniper Cole's disappearance—he almost felt sorry for the man.

But not really.

Nahum glanced over at the clock and decided it was time to call it quits for the night. He wanted to be well rested when he killed the Cole girl in the morning.

But first things first.

He needed to implement his plan—one that would seal Wyatt Scrogger's fate—and remove any possible need for the Savannah PD to continue looking for other suspects. Not that they'd find him anyway.

"Goodnight, Detective," Nahum called out.

Leo looked up and watched as Sergent Elton Nahum rolled his way into the elevator, the door sliding closed behind him.

Leo tried to like Nahum, but after six months of the man being on the job, he still possessed a palpable disdain for the crippled photographer.

For one thing, *Sergent* wasn't Nahum's rank—it was his first name—not to mention that it was spelled wrong, with the letter *a* missing. *Sergeant,* with an *a* after the second *e* was the correct spelling. What were his parents thinking?

It also bothered Leo that, though Nahum was nothing but the department photographer, the man had insisted he be allowed to carry a badge, and the chief—a total pushover—let him.

And then there was the makeup.

Maybe Nahum had acne. Maybe he was simply vain. Or maybe he was gay? Leo had no idea. All he knew was that a man wearing makeup just wasn't right.

But the final straw was the elevator.

After Nahum had interviewed for the photographer position and Leo had passed him over, Nahum threatened the department with a civil rights lawsuit, saying he was being discriminated against because of his disability. The department buckled, gave Nahum the job, and had an elevator installed. All so one man could go up and down a few times a day, and the thing was slower than shit.

The taxpayer's dollars hard at work.

*   *   *

Detective Leo Igler was sitting at his desk, reviewing the evidence, which at that moment consisted of nothing but the notes he'd taken from his interviews with Quinn Cole—Juniper Cole's highly distraught older brother—and the only person of interest in the case so far, Quinn Cole's friend Wyatt Scrogger.

Everything he'd learned so far told Leo that Wyatt Scrogger was probably involved in Juniper Cole's disappearance, if not the perpetrator himself. That would, of course, make solving the case fast and easy.

But the voice in the back of his head—and his gut instinct— told him the Scrogger kid wasn't the guy who'd taken her.

And Leo's gut was rarely wrong.

Wyatt Scrogger had answered all of Leo's questions, and he'd looked genuinely shocked when he'd been told Juniper Cole was missing. Even more, Scrogger hadn't asked for a lawyer.

But if Wyatt Scrogger hadn't taken Juniper Cole, who had?

Leo was still at his desk, shuffling papers and not doing much of anything. There was no reason to rush home; his wife had divorced him years ago, claiming that Leo—like most cops— was married to his job.

And, of course, she was right. But from personal experience, Leo Igler knew that any cop who wasn't married to the job probably wasn't getting the job done.

He opened the file again, started reading from the beginning, making sure he hadn't missed anything.

Then the phone rang.

Leo was deep in thought and ignored it.

The phone rang again.

And again.

Leo was technically off duty, and the last thing he needed right that second was to catch another case. He reached out and answered it anyway.

"Detective Igler?" a female voice asked.

"Yes, who is this?"

"My name is Glenna Thomsen-True, and I have..."

"Spell that for me," Leo said.

The woman spelled her name for Leo before continuing. *"I'm calling because I think I saw something—something strange—and it's been bothering me all day. I felt it was important to tell someone."* From the sound of the woman's voice, she was very old.

"What did you see?" Leo asked.

"Well, my husband and I are visiting friends here in Savannah, and we were heading home after dinner when we passed that big hotel, what's it called? Hang on, my husband's saying something—yes, that's it, it's called The Forsyth Park..."

Leo sat forward in his seat and asked, "The Forsyth Park Hotel?"

"Yes, that's it, on Drayton Street across from that beautiful fountain. Anyway, I saw a man helping a young girl into a brown car..."

"What time was this?" Leo asked.

"Oh, I'd say it was close to midnight."

"And what was it that made it strange?" Leo asked.

"Because the young lady, well, she looked like she was drunk. Or drugged, maybe? She could barely stand," the woman said.

"Do you remember what she was wearing?" Leo asked, feeling the hope begin to rise inside him.

"It was dark, but it was fancy—like a prom dress. I'd say it was green, or perhaps light blue?"

Bingo.

Juniper Cole had been wearing a light blue dress.

"Was there anything about the girl that stood out?" Leo asked.

"No, not really—other than her red hair, that is."

Leo knew the next question would be the big one. "Mrs. True, did you happen to write down the license plate?"

"My husband said it was probably nothing," the woman said.

Leo's heart sank.

"But he's never right about anything, so yes—I wrote it down, just in case. I have it right here in front of me."

Leo wrote down the number, repeated it back.

"Yes, that's correct," the woman said.

"I need to get the name of the people you're staying with, and a phone number where you can be reached," Leo said.

There was silence on the other end of the line.

"Well, I'm not sure that's something I'm comfortable doing, Detective," the woman said. *"We really don't want to get involved."*

"I understand, but it's important..."

The line went dead.

Leo called his contact at the Georgia Department of Motor Vehicles and told her what he needed.

The plates belonged to a 1973 Chevrolet Malibu coupe, color brown. The registered owner was Wyatt Allen Scrogger.

ORLANDO, FLORIDA
FEBRUARY 2, 2010

Dane Luckner liked being a good friend, but friendship had its limits—even when the friend was a billionaire.

Koda was behaving like a mad man. He spent nearly twenty-four hours a day sitting in front of the mirror he'd bought from the Forsyth Park Hotel.

The girl had not appeared. Not once.

And no matter what Dane said or did, it seemed impossible to get through to his friend.

Koda had neither shaved nor showered in a week.

He ignored repeated calls from his father, Bruce Mulvaney, demanding to know why he wasn't in the office.

"Talk to me, Koda. I'm on your side," Dane said again.

"Just go," Koda said finally.

"What?"

"I said, *go*," Koda repeated.

Dane didn't understand what Koda was saying. "Go? Go where?"

"Anywhere, I don't care," Koda muttered. *"Just leave."*

An hour later, Dane was packed. If Koda wanted him gone, fine. An hour after that, he was on a plane headed to New York. He hadn't seen his parents in almost two years.

It was time.

FROM THE JOURNAL OF ONYX WEBB

So much in common, you and I,
So very much the same.
Most of all, the life we choose,
With no one else to blame.

The days they pass by quickly,
The minutes faster still.
A constant search for courage—
A testing of our will.

Can we make the right decision?
Will we choose the better path?
Accept the tasks presented
Or lay calmly in the bath?

It seems we share so many things,
From love, to goals and dreams.
But like an arrow, life flies by
As water flows in streams.

So much in common, you and I,
With lives we wish to tame—
But in the end our life depends
On how we play life's game.

NEW YORK CITY
JULY 8, 1933

"It's a fairy tale!" Onyx said, gazing at the full-page ad the gallery had placed in the *New York Times* touting her first solo showing at the Schröder Gallery. Onyx's mentor, Bavarian abstract expressionist painter Hans Hoffman, would be in attendance. "But they'll be coming mostly to see Hans, not me."

"So, what if they come to meet Hoffman?" Lucas asked. "When they leave, they'll leave with a piece of Onyx." And because the crème de la crème of the New York art scene would be there, Lucas told Onyx to wear her most-glitzy dress and lots of fancy jewelry.

Onyx had neither.

*   *   *

Onyx had hoped the great German artist, Hans Hoffman, would like her work and accept her into his class. He didn't like it. He loved it.

"Extraordinary, unexplainable and indescribably original," Hoffman had said when he saw Onyx's work two years earlier, admitting her into his private study group in which many famous and notable artists took part, including Robert Beauchamp, Julius Hatofsky, Richard Stankiewicz, Anne Tabachnick, Wolf Kahn and others. Now the group also included a self-taught thirty-five-year-old woman from the swamps of Louisiana with no formal art training.

Onyx was painting every day, being challenged to develop her aesthetic eye, and she had never been happier. Then, one day, Lucas Schröder broke the news: "Hoffman says it is time to show your work to the world, Onyx. He wants you to do a solo show at the Schröder Gallery, and he plans to attend. Do you have any idea what an honor this is?"

Onyx was thrilled.

But she also knew it meant that Ulrich was going to find out she'd gone behind his back.

"If you want, I will be the one to tell him," Lucas said.

"No," Onyx said, "I'll do it myself."

*   *   *

It was the afternoon of Onyx's show at the Schröder Gallery. Onyx sat at a table at Barbetta, an upscale Italian eatery on West Forty-Sixth Street, waiting for Ulrich to arrive. She'd told him only that she wanted to celebrate some good fortune.

Onyx was a ball of nerves because of the show but also because she had no idea how Ulrich would respond to learning of her betrayal of his trust.

Twenty minutes passed then Ulrich stumbled in through the front door of the restaurant with another man—a Mohawk Indian, his head shaved on the sides and a single spiked row of black hair running up the middle of his head. Though she'd never met the man, Onyx knew he was Ulrich's drinking buddy—the one who'd gotten Ulrich his job doing construction on the Empire State building. People referred to him as Mohawk Joe. Both men were clearly drunk.

"Okay, Onyx, here I am!" Ulrich yelled. "You have something to share with me, yes?" he called out loud enough for every patron in the restaurant to turn and look in his direction.

Onyx stood up at her table. "Come have a seat, Ulrich," she said in a calm voice.

"There she *ith*," Mohawk Joe said, slurring his words and pointing a dirty finger in Onyx's direction.

Ulrich held up a copy of that day's *New York Times*, opened to the ad for Onyx's show at the gallery. "A wife does what her husband says," Ulrich said. "Are you still my wife?"

Every eye in the restaurant was on Onyx now as she walked between the tables toward where Ulrich was standing. "Yes, I am still your wife, Ulrich," Onyx said in a calm voice. "When I made my vows, I said for better or—"

Ulrich did not wait for Onyx to finish the sentence, unleashing a powerful strike to Onyx's face, her head snapping backward from the force of the blow as horrified gasps escaped from the surrounding diners.

Mohawk Joe let loose with a howl and was so unsteady from the alcohol that he fell over, grasping at a table as he went down, pulling it on top of him, plates and glasses crashing to the floor.

Onyx wanted to reach up and rub her cheek but didn't, knowing it was what Ulrich wanted.

"We are packed to leave," Ulrich said. "If you are still my wife, as you profess, you will meet us at Grand Central Terminal in one hour."

Getting on a train with her enraged husband did not sound like a good idea to Onyx. What scared her even more, however, was that Ulrich hadn't said you will be on the train with *me*...

He said us.

* * *

Lucas Schröder stood in his office in the rear of the gallery, reading the art section of *The New York Times* for the third time that morning...

> *Though the artist did not attend her own showing, the premier of works by the mysterious woman known only as "Onyx" at the Schröder Gallery was, by all accounts, the art event of the year.*

Lucas folded the article and placed it in the safe along with an envelope containing the $12,000 in cash the gallery took in from the sale of Onyx Webb's paintings the night before, every last one of them.

Onyx's failure to show up for her big night weighed heavy on him, not only because she'd missed the event—her shining moment in the sun—but also because he'd intended to tell her the reason why he'd refused to allow his brother back into the family business. The real reason.

Ulrich was a cold-blooded murderer.

This was not an opinion. Lucas knew it to be a fact because he'd watched Ulrich kill their mother with his own two hands— *he'd seen him do it with his own two eyes.*

Ulrich had claimed it was an accident, of course, but Lucas knew his younger brother was lying. Ulrich had been a compulsive liar for as long as Lucas could remember. And besides, how could a man as big as Ulrich—with hands the size of ham hocks and as strong as a vice—allow their mother to slip into the icy waters of the Atlantic Ocean?

Ulrich had her in his grasp, and then he let her slip away. No, it was not an accident—Ulrich had done it on purpose—of this Lucas was certain. Ulrich had murdered their mother.

By default, it meant that Ulrich was responsible for their father's death as well, who—when he saw his wife drop into the dark waters—jumped in after her.

There were many such stories from the night the Titanic went to its watery grave, each more devastating and tragic than the next. But this story was his. *This story was personal.*

Lucas locked the safe and turned off the lights, then wove his way through the darkened gallery, pausing at *The Veil of St. Veronica* by Gabriel von Max. Even in the dark Lucas could see Jesus's eyes open, looking directly at him, as so many visitors to the gallery had claimed to witness.

"Please protect Onyx Webb," Lucas said. "I have failed her, but you should not."

Lucas cursed himself for having waited, knowing he should have warned Onyx when he'd had the chance. Now all he had to offer was a prayer to a painting of Jesus.

He hoped it would be enough.

"We do not fear heights, we fear falling. Nor do we fear the darkness... but, rather, what we think may be lurking there. And in **matters** of life and death, we do not fear dying: only that it may be final."

The 31 Immutable Matters
of Life & Death

Episode 3
Lily Dale

This Episode Dedicated to:

M. Night Shyamalan

An amazing storyteller, you have inspired so many by developing characters people can connect with, and then devising clever twists and turns that still surprise us—even when we know they're coming.

And to the following
Onyx Webb "Super Fans"...

Adam & Rachel Chase
Sarah Spooner
Robyn C.

Written primarily to music by:

My Chemical Romance

In particular...

"Helena"
"Welcome to the Black Parade"
"I Don't Love You"
"Famous Last Words"
"Kids from Yesterday"
"S/C/A/R/E/C/R/O/W"

SAVANNAH, GEORGIA
JUNE 4, 1979

Detective Leo Igler had to make four phone calls before he was able to track down Judge Thornton Mays, who was attending a charity function at The Olde Pink House on Abercorn Street in Reynolds Square.

Leo asked the restaurant manager to get Judge Mays on the phone and was told a minute later the judge wouldn't take the call. Leo told the manager to try again, that it was an emergency, and to drag the judge to the phone if necessary.

Mays was not pleased.

"Not much of an emergency if you ask me," Mays snapped. "And you know I never sign a warrant without reviewing the evidence, Leo."

"I've got an eyewitness to the abduction, Your Honor, and time is of the essence. The perpetrator may have the Cole girl at his place right now—alive, maybe."

The fact that Leo did not know how to find the eyewitness was a detail he would deal with later.

"Bring the papers," Judge Mays said and hung up.

*　　*　　*

Judge Mays walked outside onto the front stairs of The Olde Pink House, wearing a tuxedo and holding a tall mint julep glass, waiting for Leo Igler to arrive.

Leo arrived ten minutes later, search warrant in hand. With any luck the judge hadn't changed his mind. Mays handed his drink to Leo and pulled a pair of reading glasses from his pocket. "I don't like being made to wait, Detective," Judge Mays said.

"Sorry, Your Honor," Leo said. "I got sidetracked." In truth, Leo had completely forgotten he was supposed to meet the judge.

"You got a pen?" Mays asked.

Leo dug a pen out of his jacket pocket and Mays signed the document. "You'd better be right, Leo. The only thing I hate more than waiting is being embarrassed."

Leo radioed for a small team of uniformed officers—plus Elton Nahum, the department photographer—to meet him at Wyatt Scrogger's apartment.

* * *

Sergent Elton Nahum was already there, sitting in his van, when three marked squad cars arrived at the Charlton Street address—sirens off, as instructed—parking down the street from Scrogger's single-story apartment building. Leo climbed out of the first vehicle, signaled to Nahum that it was okay to get out of the van.

"What's going on, Detective?" Nahum drawled.

"Just take pictures when I tell you, Nahum, okay?" Leo said.

Nahum shrugged. He was used to being treated like a second-class citizen by Leo Igler. However the detective wanted to play it was fine with him.

Leo looked up the street and spotted Wyatt's brown Malibu and posted an officer next to it, and then directed two more to cover the rear of the building.

With nothing else to consider, Leo Igler headed to apartment 104—accompanied by two additional officers and Nahum trailing behind in his wheelchair—with the search warrant in his hand.

Leo knocked on the door and waited. Nothing.

He pounded a bit harder, and a moment later Wyatt Scrogger opened the door, rubbing his eyes and looking as if he'd been sound asleep.

* * *

The search of Wyatt Scrogger's tiny apartment had turned up nothing, and Leo was beside himself.

"Judge Mays ain't gonna be happy," one of the cops said. Leo ignored him. The judge was the least of his problems.

The real problem was Leo had wasted the entire evening on an erroneous phone tip. And no closer to finding Juniper Cole.

"What about the car?" Nahum asked.

Christ, Nahum was right. Leo had almost forgotten to search the vehicle, which was particularly distressing since he'd gone out of his way to make sure he'd included the kid's car in the warrant.

This wasn't the only thing Leo had forgotten lately.

"May I have the keys to your vehicle?" Leo asked.

Wyatt Scrogger—who'd spent the last twenty minutes watching the entire exercise with amusement—shook his head and pulled his keys from his pocket. "You're not going to find anything there either."

Leo walked out and headed to the car with Sergent Elton Nahum rolling behind in his wheelchair. It only took a few minutes for Leo's luck to change.

"Detective, there's something you need to see," said an officer from the back of the car.

Leo walked over and looked in. The rear seat had been pulled out and lying beneath it was a plastic bag containing what looked like a pair of yellow women's panties, shoes, and an empty syringe.

"Nahum," Leo said. "Get pictures of this, okay."

"No problem, Detective. It's what I'm here to do."

"And Nahum?" Leo said quietly. "Thanks."

"My pleasure, Detective," Nahum said, pulling out his camera and going to work snapping photos.

Leo couldn't believe he'd been so careless to have almost forgotten to check the vehicle. Maybe he was losing his touch. Maybe he was losing his memory.

Or maybe he was just getting old.

SULPHUR SPRINGS, MISSOURI
AUGUST 5, 1922

"Save my baby," the injured woman said, her moans lost in the chaos of the hospital emergency room.

She was lying on a gurney, blood soaking through the dark red winter coat she had on when she was taken from the train.

"It hurts," she said through gritted teeth, breathing heavily.

"You're going to be fine," the doctor said, doing his best to put on a reassuring face.

But she would not be fine.

Her fate had already been determined.

The only thing the doctor didn't understand was how the pregnant woman survived as long as she had, considering the circumstances.

"You'll be fine," the doctor repeated, turning to the nurse. "Do we have any kind of medical history at all?"

The nurse shook her head. The woman had been brought in by ambulance, without identification, and was not from the area.

"How many months along are you?" the doctor asked over the growing symphony of wailing screams from the one-hundred-plus other train crash victims that filled every open space of the tiny hospital.

The woman lifted her head and moved her lips, but her words were unintelligible.

The doctor leaned forward, his face within inches of hers: "How far along? Six months?"

The woman in the red coat exhaled, shook her head.

"Seventh?" the doctor asked.

She shook her head again.

"Eight?"

The woman managed a slight, almost imperceptible nod.

"Eight months, okay that's good," the doctor said.

"Is there anything we can do for the pain?" the nurse asked.

The doctor ignored her. The baby was his concern, not the woman.

"What's your name?" the nurse asked the woman.

She took a deep breath, exhaled, unable to muster an answer.

The doctor could see the woman was going into shock, her eyes were glazing over as the light of her spirit began to fade.

Suddenly, the woman reached out and grabbed the doctor's arm. "Take him," she said through gritted teeth. *"Take him. Do it..."*

The woman understood. She was going to die. The only thing to be done now was to try and save the baby.

"Have you named him yet?" the nurse asked.

The woman reached up and touched the small nametag pinned to the doctor's lab coat.

The tag read: *Dr. Herman Declan.*

She tapped her finger on the name, leaving a bloody red fingerprint.

Dr. Declan managed a slight smile at the thought of such an honor, though all he wanted to do was cry.

The nurse leaned in. "And what if it's a girl?"

The woman did not answer, the light now absent from her eyes.

She was gone.

"Get me a scalpel," the doctor said sharply. "Let's at least save one damn life today."

* * *

It had been almost twenty-four hours since the first patient from the train wreck had been carried into the emergency room, and Dr. Herman Declan had managed to fight through the mental and physical exhaustion.

Until now.

Covered in blood, the doctor literally collapsed into a chair and did the only thing left to do—weep for those who'd perished, both on the tracks and on the gurneys that still surrounded him.

The nurse approached. "There's still the issue of—"

"The old woman," Dr. Declan said.

"Yes," the nurse replied.

"Is she still clutching the girl?"

The nurse nodded. "Yes, she still refuses to allow us to take her."

Dr. Declan knew the old woman should not have been allowed to keep the dead girl in her arms for so long, but with the endless parade of injured streaming in, it was the last of his priorities. Now it had to be dealt with. "What about the priest?" Dr. Declan asked.

Father Colin Fanning, who was in charge of Our Lady of the Open Arms Orphanage in the neighboring town of DeSoto, had been summoned to the hospital shortly after the crash to deliver last rites to the dead and dying.

The nurse found Father Fanning, along with Sister Mary Margaret—the head nun from the orphanage. The nurse led them to a small side room off the main building.

Though they'd been warned, both Father Fanning and Sister Mary Margaret were momentarily taken aback when they saw the condition of the girl in the old woman's arms—or what remained of her—covered in a thick layer of crusty-brown blood that had dried hours earlier.

"She was dead when they arrived," the nurse said. "But the woman refuses to let us take her."

Fanning nodded and approached the woman.

"My name is Father Fanning," he began.

The woman—who looked to be in her late seventies or early eighties perhaps—shook her head violently from side to side. "No, no, no, you will not take her, no, she's mine."

"What's her name?" Sister Mary Margaret asked.

"Lucinda," the old woman said. "This is my Lucinda."

"Do you remember being on the train?" Fanning asked.

The woman nodded. "I let her go for a drink," the old woman said. "Her car went off the tracks, but mine didn't. I searched and searched until I found her."

"It wasn't your fault. There was nothing you could do," Sister Mary Margaret said.

"But what will Titus say?" the woman asked. "My husband, he'll be home soon—from the war. He's at Gettysburg, fighting hard for the Union—and he'll want to see his Lucinda."

Father Fanning shot Sister Mary Margaret a look. "Gettysburg was a long time ago," Father Fanning said.

"Over sixty years," the old woman said, continuing to rock back and forth, as if trying to sooth the dead girl in her arms. "He isn't coming home, is he?"

"Do you realize your daughter is gone?" Father Fanning asked. "Do you understand she's gone off to be with the Lord?"

The old woman nodded. "Yes, yes, I know."

"Why don't you let Father Fanning take her so he can perform last rites?" Sister Mary Margaret said. "That way she can rest in the Lord's arms."

"Would that be okay?" Father Fanning asked.

"Could you perform the rites for all the girls?" the old woman asked.

"All the girls?" Father Fanning asked.

"Yes, for all my Lucindas," the woman said.

Father Fanning, clearly confused, turned and looked at Sister Mary Margaret. "Do you have any idea what she's talking about, Sister?"

Of course she did.

Sister Mary Margaret was three steps ahead of Father Fanning in all things, including this. He didn't even have the good sense to question why a woman of eighty claimed to have a daughter who was clearly under the age of ten.

Not only did she know who the old woman was but also knew the terrible things the woman had done.

"Not the slightest idea, Father," the nun said. "But I do believe it is our obligation to help her."

*   *   *

Once they had arrived at the Open Arms, Sister Mary Margaret helped get Obedience settled in the infirmary, while Father Fanning attended to the paperwork for the four children who would now be residing at the orphanage.

Three of the children were girls. The fourth was the newborn boy—*Declan*—named after the doctor who'd taken him from the dying woman in the red coat. No last name had been assigned. No identification had been found for the mother, who passed before doing so.

Father Fanning looked down at the infant, wrapped tightly in a white blanket and wondered about the proper procedure for assigning the boy a last name. But it was getting late and the priest was exhausted. He looked like a good Irish boy, Father Fanning thought, and wrote the first name that popped into his mind on the admittance form:

Mulvaney.

LILY DALE, NEW YORK
FEBRUARY 3, 2010

Honestly? I think it's a load of total crap," the Bulldog of a man said, his beefy arms folded across the chest of his plaid flannel shirt.

"Thomas, please," the small Maltese of a wife said from beneath the lavender shawl she'd knitted herself, something she'd started doing recently to keep her mind off of her loss.

Their loss.

"Can we just get this over with?" the Bulldog asked.

"I take it one of you is a believer, and the other is not," Ingrid Luckner said from the sofa opposite them.

"Wow, they are good," the Bulldog said sarcastically.

"Thomas, you promised," the Maltese chided.

"It's quite all right," Paul Luckner said, seated next to his wife. "We get our fair share of skeptics here at Lily Dale."

Lily Dale—or the Lily Dale Assembly, as residents call it—was a quaint town with a population of 275 in the southwestern part of New York, south of Buffalo. What made Lily Dale unique was that, in order to live there, residents had to pass a test proving their abilities as psychics, mediums, or healers of some sort. People traveled from all over the world in hopes of making contact with a loved one who had passed away.

"If you are really psychics, tell me how much money I have in my front pocket," the Bulldog said.

"Thomas, please," the Maltese implored.

"So there's no misunderstanding, Paul and I are not psychics," Ingrid said.

"That's right," Paul continued, following a well-rehearsed script the two of them had used for going on thirty years. "Ingrid and I are trained mediums."

"I didn't realize there was a difference," the Maltese said.

"Oh, yes. Psychics use tools like crystal balls or tarot cards to see the future," Paul said.

"Mediums—like us—communicate with those who have passed on, usually through spirit guides that act as a bridge between the physical world and spiritual world," Ingrid added.

"Like that John Edward fellow?" the Maltese asked.

Paul and Ingrid stiffened in unison and forced smiles to hide their jealousy. It was hard to ignore the success of celebrity mediums who achieved fame with their own cable TV shows, speaking to packed ballrooms of believers eagerly shelling out $150 a head to be there.

"We prefer a quieter existence, out of the limelight," Paul Luckner said.

"So, if you're expecting us to tell you which lottery numbers to play or which pony to bet on at the track, you'll be disappointed in our time together," Ingrid said, moving the conversation forward. "But if your goal is to make contact with someone who has passed on..."

"Yes, that's what we want," the Maltese said, tears welling up in her eyes. "My husband and I are here to make contact with..."

"Christ, honey, don't tell their names," the Bulldog said, cutting his wife off mid-sentence.

"Your husband is right," Paul said. "You do not need to share any details with us. In fact, we'd prefer that you didn't."

The Bulldog pulled a handkerchief from his pocket and handed it to the Maltese. "Will they come through?" the Maltese asked, dabbing her eyes.

"The veil separating the living and the dead is very thin," Ingrid said. "If a loved one wishes to communicate, he or she will."

"That said, it helps if you keep an open mind," Paul added, looking directly at the Bulldog. "Now, if you're ready, we'll start the recording."

*   *   *

Paul and Ingrid sat in silence, eyes closed. "Your daughter is passed," Ingrid said finally, not as a question but as a statement of fact.

The Maltese placed her hand to her chest, looked at her husband. "Our daughter?"

"Yes, she... she says she's sorry," Ingrid continued. "Sally? No, Sandy."

"Oh," the Maltese gasped.

"Marcus wants you to know he's here, too," Paul said.

The Bulldog leaned forward in his chair.

"Oh, my God," the Maltese managed through a stream of steadily falling tears. "They're together. Sandy and Marcus are together. Are they okay?"

Paul Luckner rocked back and forth, eyes tightly closed as if working hard to listen to a voice from a great distance. "He says, not her fault. His fault. Drinking. Too many drinks."

"Damn right it was his fault," the Bulldog said.

"It happened so fast, your daughter says. There was no time, she couldn't help it," Ingrid said.

"Help what?" the Maltese asked.

"She's showing me an animal, a deer," Ingrid continued, her eyes tightly closed, head tilted to the side. "So fast, no time, so fast, no time, so fast, no time."

"This is total bullshit!" the Bulldog snorted. "Where did you get this? From some Internet search? You got it wrong, my daughter wasn't driving. She wasn't! It was that drunken husband of hers!"

"Stop!" the Maltese screamed. "It's our daughter. I need to hear this!"

"Sandy is showing me the keys. She is saying she took the keys. She says that she was driving. '*So sorry, so sorry, so so so so sorry,*' Sandy keeps saying, '*so so sorry.*'"

The Bulldog dropped his head, and the tears began to come—held back for months.

Oddly, the Maltese was suddenly stoic, as if the two had inexplicably changed roles. "Our daughter, Sandy—and her husband, Marcus—were killed in a car crash two months ago, coming home from a party," the Maltese said calmly. "They hit a tree. Both were thrown from the vehicle so no one knew for sure who was driving."

"We assumed it was him, Marcus," the Bulldog said, regaining his composure. "Marcus drank a lot. I told Sandy not to get in the car with him if he'd had too much, to take the keys from him if..."

"Marcus is sorry for his weakness, for his mistakes. He's asking for your forgiveness," Paul said.

The Maltese nodded. "Of course. Of course we do." She put her arms around the Bulldog and held the big man in her arms as he began to sob.

"They know how sad you both are, and they came through to tell you they are okay, and you must live. As hard as it sounds, know that they are always with you, but you must live," Ingrid said.

"Can you tell them that...?"

Paul shook his head. "They're gone," he said. "But don't worry, they know. They know."

*   *   *

The Bulldog wrote out a check for $250 and hugged Paul for the third time. "We can't thank you enough," he said, and then hugged them both again.

Paul opened the door and saw the couple out, then joined Ingrid in the kitchen as she made a pot of tea. "That was a difficult one," Ingrid said.

"Yes, it was," Paul said. "Nothing can ever take the pain away, not entirely, but knowing your loved ones are okay and at peace brings enormous comfort."

There was a knock on the door.

"Looks like someone I know is going to get another hug," Ingrid said with a giggle. Paul made his way to the door, swung it open and saw his son standing there, suitcase in hand.

"Dane!" Paul exclaimed as he stepped out onto the porch and hugged his son. "Why didn't you call? We would have picked you up." Paul took the suitcase from Dane's hand and ushered him inside, then called out. "Ingrid! Our son is home!"

Dane heard his mother scream with joy from the kitchen.

An hour later, Dane settled in his room, exhausted.

He laid on his bed, looking around at his things—photos, yearbooks, lacrosse trophies, clothes hanging in the closet just as he'd left them almost two years earlier—and wondered if he could ever resign himself to such a simple existence again.

Two years traveling the world in a private jet, staying in the best hotels, being ushered into clubs like an A-list celebrity had changed him.

He was not the same little kid who'd grown up in Lily Dale.

But he wasn't part of that other world either. Not really.

He'd been spoiled by treatment that never would have been afforded him had he not been Koda Mulvaney's friend.

Dane closed his eyes. *Who am I without Koda? Am I anyone? Do I even exist?*

The thought scared him. He felt lost.

Dane felt something thump on the bottom of the bed near his feet. He opened his eyes and saw a small brown and white terrier standing there, tail wagging, looking at him expectantly.

"Hey, Duffy," Dane said. "I missed you, boy."

The dog offered a tiny snort then jumped off the bed and ran toward the closed door.

And directly through it.

The fact that Dane's childhood dog had just run through a solid object didn't faze him in the least. He was used to such things growing up in Lily Dale.

LAS VEGAS, NEVADA
JULY 8, 1933

Onyx had been presented with a tough choice: Stay in New York and follow her dream of becoming a successful painter, or leave with her husband.

She left with Ulrich.

The deciding factor was the specific part of her wedding vows—the *'till death do us part* phrase—which Onyx took very seriously.

Once the Twentieth Century Limited departed Grand Central Terminal, Onyx made it clear to Ulrich that should he ever so much as raise his hand to her again—in public or in private—it would be the end of the marriage. She also insisted he stop drinking.

The days that followed were even harder than Onyx anticipated as the exhilarating high of the Big Apple gave way to the depressing reality of the new destination Ulrich had chosen for them: A place called Las Vegas.

The good news was that Mohawk Joe was not coming with them, opting to get off the train in Chicago where the Indian had a line on a job working on the Twenty-Second Street sewer tunnel project. Based on the way the man smelled, it seemed totally appropriate. A few months earlier, a number of workers had been trapped thirty-five-feet below earth in the tunnel, several dying of smoke inhalation when a fire broke out. Since then, getting workers for the project proved difficult.

The Mohawk was not concerned.

A fierce and fearless tribe, the Mohawks accepted any kind of work, usually involving dangerous conditions—bridges, skyscrapers, tunnels, it didn't matter—often at below-average, non-union wages.

In that way, Mohawk Joe and Ulrich were birds of a feather. Fortunately, the drunken Indian got off the train in Chicago as planned.

SAVANNAH, GEORGIA
JUNE 5, 1979

The big question, Sergent Elton Nahum thought to himself as he carried a three-foot tall, cylindrical glass container down the staircase was: *Why had he kept Juniper alive so long?* He hadn't intended to.

When the truth hit him, he refused to acknowledge it, but the truth was the truth. Or, as his mother used to say, *"Lying lips are an abomination to the Lord, but those who act faithfully are His delight."* She'd say things like that all the time, having been raised on a farm in the middle of Wisconsin by fanatically religious parents who controlled her every move. At least, that's how she described his grandparents.

So she ran away and got knocked up at the age of sixteen, became a stripper and was beaten to death by the club owner for stealing money from the safe.

Everybody's got a story, right?

Nahum placed the glass container on a metal rolling cart and, for safe measure, secured the container to the cart with bungee cord. The last thing he needed now was to break the only glass container he had—if he did he'd need to keep the girl alive for another two or three days until a replacement arrived.

And that could be dangerous.

He was becoming attached to the girl as it was.

Okay, *attached* might be a bit of an overstatement, Nahum thought as he wheeled the container through the one-hundred-yard-long dark tunnel.

He'd bought the house with no idea the tunnel even existed, discovering it by accident when he was preparing his secret room in the basement. Based on where the tunnel led, Nahum assumed it had been built during the civil war, presumably by slaves who were connecting the main plantation house to the slave quarters. Maybe they used it to move food back and forth or were planning an escape. He really didn't care what the reason had been. He was simply glad it existed, making his secret place all the more secret.

Nahum rolled the cart with the glass container into the room where Juniper was being held, still lying on her back, secured to the metal table with leather straps. Nahum didn't bother addressing her—he wasn't there to talk. He was there to prepare.

Juniper had other plans.

"What is that for?" Juniper asked.

Nahum unstrapped the glass container from the roller cart and set it on a nearby table, then left. Ten minutes later, Nahum returned—this time with a brown box—which he set on the floor.

"What are you planning to do to me?" Juniper asked. "I want to know."

"What I have to do," Nahum replied.

"What you *have* to do?" Juniper said. "No one *has* to do anything."

"Ah, but that's where you're wrong," Nahum said. "There are many things a person must do in this world, many of them things we wish we didn't have to. Go to school, go to work, walk the dog, brush our teeth before we go to bed. The list is endless."

"I'm not talking about those things," Juniper said. "I'm talking about—"

Nahum turned to her. "What I'm going to do is not nearly as important as why. You already know *what* I'm going to do—and you already know there is nothing you can do to stop it from happening. I would think the thing you'd want to know is why?"

"Okay," Juniper said. *"Why are you doing this?"*

"I tell you what, Juniper," Nahum said. "I'm going to show you something no one else has ever seen."

"What is it?"

"My collection," Nahum said. "I've been putting it together since the age of six. Do you want to see it?"

"I'm not—okay, yes," Juniper said. Part of her didn't want to see whatever he was going to show her, but then she realized as long as she was doing as he asked, maybe there was still a chance.

Nahum walked over, grabbed the metal table with Juniper on it, and rolled it to the other side of the small room where a curtain hung like a partition. He grabbed a latch on the side of the table and pulled it, adjusting the table from a horizontal position to an almost vertical one, so Juniper was upright. Then he grabbed the end of the curtain and pulled it back.

"Take a look, Juniper," Nahum said. "You want to know what I'm going to do to you, and more importantly, why? You're a smart girl. Figure it out."

MURPHYSBORO, ILLINOIS
MARCH 18, 1925

Thomas Bilazzo had driven this particular delivery route for the Murphysboro Milk Company for so long he was pretty sure he could do it with his eyes closed, which was something he wished he could do at that very moment.

God, he was tired.

His first child—Tommy Bilazzo Junior—had been born two weeks earlier, and getting a full night's sleep had been impossible ever since. It wasn't like he could simply stay in bed while his wife tended to the parental duties. She worked just as long and hard as he did, maybe more so. Returning to her job as a fourth grade school teacher after only three days of rest, Luisa had to deal with the demands of twenty-six students as well.

But, Christ, he was tired.

Thomas glanced down at his watch. It was 2:43 in the afternoon. He was fifteen minutes ahead of schedule. Certainly there would be no harm in simply closing his eyes for just ten minutes. He steered the truck to the side of the road and turned off the engine. Ten good minutes was all he needed, he told himself, closing his eyes and relaxing back in his seat.

And that's when he heard the sound.

It started as a deep hum, making him think he hadn't turned off the motor. But he knew he had. Thomas opened his eyes, and there—on the distant horizon—he saw what could best be described as low rolling clouds, boiling up from the soil like ash erupting from a volcano. He sat upright and rubbed his eyes.

Then, from behind the cloud of dust, it became visible: A behemoth of a funnel cloud, a twister unlike anything he'd ever laid eyes on.

He reached for the key and started the engine as the low-grade hum grew into a vibrating rumble, which escalated quickly into an ear-shattering roar. The wind began pushing dust at him, the front edge of the giant cloud swirling in front of him, throwing rocks, sticks and leaves.

He knew he needed to go. But where? Where could he go? The storm was all around him now, coming down on him like a freight train and twice as loud.

Thomas looked over at the small basket on the passenger seat, a basket with a sleeping little boy in it, tucked under a small blanket.

Today had been Thomas's scheduled day off. But then the phone had rung. Someone had called out sick. Could he cover the route? His first instinct was to say that he couldn't, but the thought of the extra income from the overtime was simply too enticing.

Now, here he was with no options.

Then Thomas had an idea.

*　*　*

Ninety-seven miles northwest, Katherine Keane sat up on the sofa in the living room of her small St. Louis apartment, finding it almost impossible to breathe, fear and panic welling up in her chest.

It happened again.

She just had another vision.

The visions had started twenty-one years earlier, shortly after she'd died and then been saved—or, resurrected—in Obedience Everhardt's storm cellar.

And they'd never stopped.

Every few weeks she'd wake up in a panic, as she had just now, thinking she'd simply had a bad dream. And if anyone was entitled to a bad dream here and there, it was Katherine. Being held for six years as a prisoner in a crazy woman's basement—a crazy woman who'd hit her in the mouth with a ball-peen hammer, knocking out several teeth and scaring her for life—will do that to someone.

But these weren't normal dreams. They were visions in which Katherine would literally be inside another person, seeing the world through their eyes and living their experience, including their fear, panic and pain.

This time, she'd been napping in the front seat of a delivery truck when the rumbling of a tornado awakened her. The sight of the mammoth twister bearing down on her caused fear as thick as bile to rise in her throat, something she was all too familiar with.

Looking down, she could see her hands on the truck's steering wheel and knew the person in the front seat—the person she was inside—was a man.

On the seat next to him was a small baby, a newborn. A boy, no more than a few weeks old.

Katherine could feel the man's love for the boy. She also could hear him thinking the boy's name over and over again.

Tommy. Tommy. Tommy.

Tommy Bilazzo Junior, named after his father.

It was as though his thoughts were her own. He quickly reviewed his options. None of them were good. There was nowhere to go... nowhere to run... nowhere to hide.

Maybe they could get under the truck?

Then, the thought of the large metal milk cans—the ones he delivered full of milk to the commercial accounts, to hospitals and restaurants—entered his mind.

There were several empty ones in back.

Thomas snatched the basket containing his son and jumped from the truck, the winds so strong he could barely fight his way through it, sticks and stones ripping at his skin.

At her skin, too.

He reached the back of the truck and swung the door open, exposing two rows of large metal milk cans. One row of cans was filled with milk, but the cans in the other row were empty.

He grabbed one of the empty cans, the truck rocking violently from side to side, and opened it. Then he lifted his young baby boy from the basket and placed him into the empty can.

Yes, Katherine thought. *This is good. Don't worry, Thomas, God will take it from here.*

Hold onto the can, Katherine could hear Thomas Bilazzo thinking. *No matter what, don't let go of the can.*

No, Katherine thought, *let go. Let go!*

She felt the man's hands begin to release their grip on the can, knowing he could hear her just as she could hear him. But his human instincts would not let him, nor would his instincts as a father.

Thomas tightened his grip on the can again, trying to hold on as the roar of the twister battered his eardrums, the full brunt of the windy beast only seconds from reaching the truck.

It's going to be fine, Katherine thought loudly. *Let go and let God handle it. Trust God, have trust in Him and just let go!*

"I love you, son," Thomas said aloud. "And you, Luisa, my darling wife. I love you both so very much." And then, in an act of pure faith, Thomas Bilazzo released his grip and allowed the force of the wind to rip the can from his hands, hurling it upward into the black, swirling sky.

Katherine was still breathing heavily when she climbed from the sofa and went to the small kitchen of her apartment for some water. Then she grabbed a pad of paper and a pencil to write down the man's name.

And the message—*Tommy Bilazzo.*

During every vision, there was always a message; a message she had come to trust over the years.

She didn't worry about the spelling being correct, for she knew it would be. God didn't make mistakes. Ever.

Then she wrote down the message God had sent:

Our Lady of the Open Arms.

ORLANDO, FLORIDA
FEBRUARY 4, 2010

There were four elevators in the main lobby area of the 55 West building. Three ran from the ground floor to the thirtieth floor, with a button for each floor in between.

The fourth was a private elevator that went from the lobby directly to the penthouse on the thirty-first floor—with no other stops—and required a key.

Koda heard the elevator doors slide open but did not move.

He was lying on the sofa, an episode of *The Real World: New Orleans* on the sixty-inch flat screen TV, the sound muted. Koda knew little about the long-running reality series and nothing about any of the characters.

And he didn't care.

He wasn't watching the television—he was watching the mirror mounted next to it.

Mika Flagler entered and surveyed the array of empty pizza boxes, crumpled-up Jimmy John's sandwich bags, and a half-dozen empty Tito's vodka bottles.

"You know your mailbox is full, right?" Mika said.

Koda shrugged and said nothing.

Mika began rummaging through the mess, finally locating Koda's iPhone under a cushion at the end of the sofa. She grabbed it and navigated her way to Koda's voicemail.

Five of the calls were from her.

Delete.

Six calls were from Koda's father, Bruce, no doubt telling Koda to get his ass back to work.

Delete.

Some of the calls were from Dane.

Definitely delete.

The only call of any interest was from someone at TMZ who'd been tipped that Koda was living in Orlando. While the majority of celebrities considered TMZ, and other paparazzi-based outfits to be a nuisance, Mika considered them essential to her goals.

Save.

"Get dressed. We're going out," Mika said.

"How'd you get up here?" Koda asked, eyes still fixed on the mirror.

"I got the keys from your father," Mika said. "He's very concerned about you."

"My father is worried about me?"

"Okay, check that," Mika said. "He's pissed as hell."

Koda shrugged and said nothing.

Mika grabbed several empty sandwich bags and walked over to a garbage can and stuffed them in. "What happened to your maid service?"

"I don't want them here," Koda said. "I don't want you here either."

"You can't send me away like you did Dane," Mika said. "I'm not some old college pal. I'm your fiancé."

"I don't remember proposing again," Koda said.

"Don't worry, you will," Mika said.

In so many ways, Koda Mulvaney was less than the perfect choice for Mika's needs. He wasn't ambitious, lacking anything that resembled a work ethic. He wasn't faithful and made no attempt to hide his indiscretions. And while Koda was far from dumb, he wasn't going to be invited to join Mensa anytime soon, either.

But in the two areas that really mattered, Koda was perfect for her. First—even though he'd managed to run through his initial $20 million trust fund in less than two years—he would have access to $2 billion when he reached the age of twenty-five. And second, he was gorgeous and looked great on Mika's arm.

But this mirror thing was starting to get on her nerves.

"So, has this ghost girl of yours shown up again?"

Koda shook his head.

"Maybe it was..."

"She was real, Mika," Koda barked.

"I believe you, honey," Mika said, though in truth she really didn't. "I was about to say maybe it was a one-time thing. You know, like a drive-by haunting."

Mika sat down on the sofa next to Koda, took his hand and placed it in hers. "You look like hell and you've got to eat. If this girl is real, she can come back after dinner."

Koda didn't understand why, but his heart ached to see the girl again. But Mika was right, he had to eat.

Mika leaned in and kissed Koda on the cheek. "Shave, okay?"

Mika waited until Koda closed the bedroom door behind him and then grabbed his iPhone and pressed the number for TMZ.

"Wear your blue Bugatti shirt," Mika called out. "It matches your eyes."

Blue also photographed extremely well.

LAS VEGAS, NEVADA
SEPTEMBER 8, 1934

as Vegas was even worse than Onyx had anticipated. She and Ulrich had been in the city for over a year, and things weren't getting any better. The city was small, dirty, and filled with men desperate for work like her husband.

The only paved thoroughfare in Las Vegas—Fremont Street—had just installed the city's first traffic light. She'd gone from being free to roam a city that had everything to being trapped in a dust-filled hell-hole in the middle of nowhere.

Of course, Ulrich had picked Las Vegas for the same reason he picked every place they'd ever lived—because he could get work. In this case, it was on the dam being built at the direction of President Herbert Hoover. Again, it would be Ulrich's unique background as a trapeze artist that would have him earning a living at terrifying heights.

When they arrived, the city was in the throes of chaos. The state legislature had just legalized gaming, which led to an overnight explosion of bars, casinos and showgirl theaters. Most were controlled by the Chicago mob and designed to entertain workers who flooded the town on weekends in pursuit of the three G's: *gin, girls and gambling.*

The most dangerous of the three was definitely gambling. Too much gin, you simply passed out. Too many girls? Yes, if one had too many girls, you would pass out from exhaustion.

But gambling?

Gambling was different.

No matter how long you gambled, you could always gamble more—especially when you were winning. Of course, for many, they would never win because they couldn't quit.

Nothing could wipe away a week's pay faster than gambling, and if a shylock got their hooks into you, your last paycheck was the least of your problems. The rule was simple—*pay your debts or pay with your legs.*

Or worse.

It was a lesson Ulrich was forced to learn the hard way.

When he wasn't working out at the dam, Ulrich could be found at the poker tables in one of three places on Fremont Street: Club 21, the Northern Club, or the aptly named Las Vegas Club.

"All smart gamblers play poker," Ulrich told Onyx when they first arrived in town. "I just need a bankroll to get started."

"Aren't the odds always in the house's favor?" Onyx asked.

"With roulette and the slots, yes," Ulrich contended. "But poker? No, with poker you aren't playing against the house, you are playing against the biggest sucker at the table." Amazingly, for a while, Ulrich proved to be quite the poker player, winning a significant amount from fellow workers.

Then Ulrich fell off the wagon.

Unfortunately, once Ulrich had a few gins in him, the biggest sucker at the table on most nights turned out to be him, and he was too drunk to realize it. Within six months, Ulrich's winnings were depleted and he took his first loan from Hyman Holtz, a shylock who went by the nickname "The Hammer" and operated from the rear of a barbershop next door to the Majestic Theater.

"The vigorish is 20 percent, you understand what that means?" The Hammer asked.

Ulrich didn't.

The *vigorish*—commonly referred to as *the vig* for short—was a complicated means of calculating the interest rate being charged on the loan.

"No problem," Ulrich said, signing the marker but ignoring the question. "I'll have your money back in two days."

He didn't.

It wasn't long before Ulrich was forced to borrow from Frankie "Fingers" Agnello to pay off The Hammer... and from Pauly "The Pinch" DeFeo to repay Fingers... and then from Bennie "The Knife" Juliano. Worst of all, though, was Faustino

"The Owl" Spilatro, to whom Ulrich currently owed $900, with the vig making the total grow larger by the day.

The Owl had given Ulrich three days to come up with the cash or he'd send his sons to collect the hard way.

That had been a week ago.

* * *

While Ulrich was busy running up gambling debts, Onyx worked waiting tables at the Apache to men with dirty hands downing shots of gin and bourbon into the wee hours of the morning. It was not what Onyx considered fulfilling work, but the tips were good and they paid the rent.

A year earlier, not long after Onyx and Ulrich arrived, movie star Marlene Dietrich—who'd just finished shooting *The Scarlet Empress* in Hollywood—had passed through. She'd been invited by Las Vegas mobster Meyer Lansky to make a stop in the dusty little town in an attempt to put the city on the map with other Hollywood-types. Had Dietrich seen the town before saying yes, she might not have agreed.

Onyx stood near the side of the stage that night and watched as Dietrich—wearing a top hat, a white blouse under a tight grey vest, and silk stockings—took command of the room. Dietrich was everything a woman could and should be, Onyx thought— audacious, magnetic, witty, charming, and seductive—someone who grabbed the world by the collar and took it with her wherever she went. Most of all, Marlene Dietrich was a liberated woman. And that was the moment Onyx decided to take her life back.

"I think I would like to try my hand at singing," she told Ulrich when she arrived home that night.

"You think you can become Marlene Dietrich?" Ulrich asked. "You're not even very good at being Onyx Schröder."

"Webb," Onyx said.

"What?"

Onyx had just used her maiden name for the first time in six years, and it felt good. "You heard me."

"All of a sudden my name is no longer good enough for you?"

Onyx remained silent.

Ulrich took a step toward her, but he knew better than to raise a hand to his Onyx after she promised to leave him if he ever touched her again.

Ulrich simply turned and stormed from the room.

*   *   *

Ulrich walked down Fremont Street in desperate need of a drink. He couldn't show his face in any of his favorite haunts for fear of running into one of the many loan sharks he owed money.

He turned left, worked his way down Ogden all the way to Ninth Street where he spotted a place called The Night Owl. He took a seat at the bar and put back two quick shots of bourbon, then ordered a third.

"You have driven me to drink, Onyx Webb," Ulrich said aloud to no one in particular.

"Let me guess," the female voice came from behind him. Ulrich turned to see a curvaceous cigarette girl standing there. "Lucky Strikes, right?"

Smoking was one of the few vices Ulrich did not partake in, but the stunning girl caught him off guard. "Yes, Lucky Strikes," he said.

Two hours later, Ulrich was lying on his back, blowing smoke at the ceiling as the naked cigarette girl drew circles on his chest with a painted nail.

"My name is Claudia," the girl said casually, "in case you're wondering."

He wasn't. Ulrich was thinking about how deeply in debt he was to the loan sharks and contemplating his options.

"You want to see a picture of my favorite place in the whole wide world?" Claudia said, rolling over and grabbing her purse. Ulrich took the small black-and-white photo from Claudia's hand.

It was a picture of a lighthouse, set majestically on top of a cliff, the Pacific Ocean in the background with waves crashing the shore below.

"It's called Crimson Cove," Claudia said. "I grew up there, on the Oregon coast. It's the type of romantic place a couple could go and simply disappear forever.

FROM THE JOURNAL OF ONYX WEBB

It is important to understand that ghosts have always walked among us, among The Living. And not just ghosts of the Now-You-See-Them, Now-You-Don't variety, who show up as gray wisps that appear and then just as quickly disappear, but fully-formed, fully-energized ghosts who look just as human as you and others...

Ghosts who live undetected, toiling away in jobs they tolerate, riding the bus to and from prisons of their own making ...

Ghosts who serve our dinners in restaurants and clean our houses and perhaps even babysit our children.

Ghosts who, if you're not paying close attention—or should you not know what to look for—appear and sound and "feel" to the touch like the living.

Well, almost.

Of course, this can be disconcerting for some people to learn. But, rest assured that over time I will share everything you need to know...

Every telltale sign to look for...

And in the case of the few dark ghosts who walk among the living, I will tell you everything you need to fear.

SAVANNAH, GEORGIA
JUNE 5, 1979

The man had been gone for ten minutes, leaving Juniper in front of what looked like a shrine comprised of an eclectic assortment of items.

Juniper had no idea what to make of it. It was like a giant puzzle, but none of the pieces seemed to connect.

The wall itself was covered with photographs, mostly of Ferris wheels. Most of the Ferris wheels Juniper had ever seen were huge, with big cars you climbed into. These all seemed small, like something you'd see at a country fair—with chairs you sat in, your legs dangling free below.

In addition to the photos, there was also a collection of models of Ferris wheels, sitting on shelves on the wall—possibly antiques.

Then there were the newspaper articles, one with a picture of a large Ferris wheel. It was the front page of the *St. Louis Post-Dispatch*, yellow with age, from August of 1904. The headline read:

ST. LOUIS CHILD SNATCHER
FOUND—TWO GIRLS SAVED
BUT KILLER ESCAPES

Beneath the photo of the Ferris wheel was a photo of two young girls, one a bit older than the other. Juniper couldn't read the details of the article, and could just barely make out the caption:

> *Two lucky girls! Katherine Keane, age 12, of St. Louis (left), and Onyx Webb, age 6, of Louisiana, survivors.*

The girls' names meant nothing to Juniper. She needed to move on, turning her attention to another article, this one from the *Waukesha Daily Freeman*, with a headline reading:

JURY AWARDS $2.3 MILLION TO
WISCONSIN FARM ACCIDENT VICTIM

The balance of items appeared to be the typical assortment of things a kid would have in their room.

A blue and silver "First Place" ribbon with track runner on it.

An old black and white Polaroid photo of a woman in a cocktail waitress outfit that looked like it was from the 1950s or '60s.

A color photo of a boy and a girl in their teens, taken at a prom or dance of some kind. Even though the boy in the photo was ten years younger, Juniper could tell it was the man who'd taken her.

Over in the corner were stacks of what looked like comic books, record albums, and board games.

What did it all mean?

Juniper turned her attention to what was in the center of it all: The table with the empty cylindrical glass container the man had brought in earlier.

An empty glass container.

The container was tall, at least three-feet high. And it was wide—tall enough and wide enough to fit half of a person.

Half a person.

Juniper looked at the box the man had set beneath the table and read what was printed on the side: *Formaldehyde 40%, APC Pure. 6 - One Gallon Bottles.*

Juniper looked back at the pictures of the Ferris wheels on the wall. All the photos were of old-time Ferris wheels—the kind from the '50s and '60s where you sat in a swing with your legs dangling free below—and she understood.

The pictures weren't of the Ferris wheels.

They were pictures of legs.

* * *

Ninety minutes later it was over.

Nahum finished cleaning the floor and the metal table, removed his rubber gloves and placed them in a plastic trash bag and sealed it. Then he pulled a chair into the center of the room and took a seat. He hadn't figured out exactly where to dispose of everything, but he could do it later. Right now he just wanted to sit and enjoy his work.

Juniper Cole was his fourth victim.

The first time he'd killed a girl, it was in a fit of blind rage, but he hadn't thought things through. He hadn't even considered taking her legs.

The second time was in Myrtle Beach, South Carolina. He'd strangled the girl in a hotel room, panicked, and simply left her there.

The third kill was also in a hotel room—in Charleston. He'd managed to get the woman's legs, but a cop car turned the corner as he was carrying them to the van. So he did the only thing he could—he dropped them in the middle of the street and ran.

In retrospect, he was lucky to get away.

Nahum vowed then and there that the next time he would do it right. And he had.

The only question now was:

Would one pair of legs be enough?

DESOTO, MISSOURI
MARCH 23, 1925

t had been almost three years since Obedience Everhardt had been found among the survivors of the Sulphur Springs train tragedy that had taken thirty-four lives and injured another 186 men, women and children.

Sister Mary Margaret had recognized the old woman with the long gray pony tail immediately—but she pretended otherwise. Then she talked Father Fanning into taking the traumatized old woman with them to the orphanage, and the priest reluctantly agreed.

But why had she done it?

Why had Sister Mary Margaret gone out of her way to keep Obedience Everhardt's identity a secret? It was a question the nun had asked herself numerous times. Then one day it hit her.

It was curiosity.

She was curious to learn about the woman. In particular, she wanted to hear about the girls Obedience had taken and killed. She had never met anyone else who had killed before, at least not to her knowledge.

In Sister Mary Margaret's case, however, it was boys. Maybe she and Obedience were merely opposite sides of the same coin.

Sister Mary Margaret had long wondered if the old woman would ever come clean and admit who she was, but she never did. So the nun began working Obedience for information about her past but to no avail. The old woman pretended to have no memory before that day on the train, but Sister Mary Margaret knew it was an act. What Obedience shared that day at the emergency room had been the result of trauma, not a desire to confess.

So, as Sister Mary Margaret and Obedience took their usual afternoon walk in the woods, the nun turned and said, "I know who you are, Obedience Everhardt, and I know the terrible things you've done."

Obedience stopped, a look of genuine surprise on her face. "When did...?"

Sister Mary Margaret pulled a pack of Old Gold's from a secret pocket sewn on the inside of her habit. She shook one of the unfiltered cigarettes loose from the pack and lit it.

"When?" the nun said, taking a seat on a fallen tree at the edge of the woods. "The first day in the emergency room. What, you think that just because I'm a nun that I don't read the daily paper?"

"Does Father Fanning know?" Obedience asked.

Sister Mary Margaret inhaled deeply, then blew a long stream of blue smoke into the air. "Father Fanning is an idiot."

"Why didn't you turn me over to the police?"

"Do you think I should have?"

"I would think you would have," Obedience said. "After all, I have committed sins. Murder. The worst sin of all."

"Where did you ever get the idea that the church is in the business of punishment?" Sister Mary Margaret said. "We're in the business of forgiveness."

Obedience said nothing.

"Do you feel guilt over what you've done?" Sister Mary Margaret asked.

"Yes," Obedience said, "a great, suffocating guilt that chokes the remaining life from me daily."

"Well, Obedience, this is your lucky day," Sister Mary Margaret said, taking another drag from her Old Gold and making the sign of the cross. "I forgive you of your sins."

"What about God?" Obedience asked. "Will God forgive me?"

Sister Mary Margaret thought for a moment.

"It would have been better if you'd taken boys. Girls are angels, but boys? Boys are little more than rodents."

"I thought God looked down at all his creatures the same," Obedience said.

Sister Mary Margaret took one last drag from the Old Gold and snuffed it out on the log. "Yes, God is very good that way, Obedience. But God doesn't have to take their shit all day, now does he?"

* * *

The next morning Sister Mary Margaret was standing at the front of a classroom, teaching a history lesson, when a young girl began wailing.

"Look over there! Look over there!" the girl screamed.

"What is the meaning of this?" Sister Mary Margaret demanded.

"There, in the woods!" the girl said, pointing out the window.

Several kids jumped from their seats and ran to the window.

"Children, take your seats!" Sister Mary Margaret yelled as she crossed the room toward them.

The children scrambled quickly back to their desks as Sister Mary Margaret approached the window and looked out.

"What is it? I do not see anything."

"There, in the trees," the young girl said, pointing again. "The woman in the trees."

Sister Mary Margaret looked again, following the girl's pointed finger and finally saw her.

It was Obedience Everhardt—a rope pulled tightly around her neck—hanging from the branch of a large oak.

LILY DALE, NEW YORK
FEBRUARY 5, 2010

Why didn't you bring Koda with you?" Ingrid Luckner asked from across the kitchen, removing the remaining strips of bacon from a well-worn black-iron skillet.

Dane had been home for less than twelve hours and was already regretting the decision. Then again, where else was he going to go?

Growing up behind the picturesque gates of the tiny village, established in 1879 on the eastern shore of Cassadaga Lake, had been both a blessing and a curse.

On Dane's fifth birthday, his parents had taken him to the lake for a picnic. They'd just sat down at a table in the gazebo when Dane excitedly asked, *"Can we go on the Ferris wheel?"*

"Ferris wheel?" his father said, looking expectantly to Dane's mother.

"Are there people on the Ferris wheel?" his mother asked.

"Sure, lots of them," Dane replied.

"Can you tell us what the people look like?" his father asked.

"They're wearing hats and holding umbrellas," Dane had replied.

Paul and Ingrid Luckner shared a knowing look, then hugged Dane tightly. Yes, he shared their gift.

The Ferris wheel had been torn down a hundred years earlier.

Dane had no idea what all the fuss was about. But his parents seemed happy, and that was a good thing.

But the curse of living in Lily Dale was how Dane was treated in school—taunted and bullied—called everything from creep-boy to freak-fest, and other things too vile to repeat.

In particular, Dane remembered the day in fifth grade when a classmate said, *"Hey, Houdini, wanna read my palm?"* Dane wittily responded: *"Houdini wasn't a psychic. He was a magician... ass-wipe."* At which point Dane had the crap beat out of him.

"So, what is Koda up to these days?" his father asked.

What to say?

There was a part of Dane that wanted to tell them about Koda's situation—about seeing a girl in a mirror, a girl he thought looked dead. On the other hand, when Dane went off to college he'd pledged to never tell a soul about his spiritualist roots— growing up in Lily Dale—or that his mother and father communicated with the dead for a living.

"I need to take a walk," Dane said.

*   *   *

Dane grabbed his Syracuse University letterman's jacket and a scarf and headed out the door toward the frozen lake. He walked passed row after row of quiet streets lined with quaint, snow-dusted gingerbread houses, feeling like an outsider in the only home he'd ever known.

He wound his way along the path through Leolyn Woods and past "Inspiration Stump," where mediums still held outdoor services twice a day during the summer months.

Dane made his way to the pet cemetery where residents of Lily Dale had been saying good-bye to their beloved companions for over a hundred years. He found the little marker he and his father had made together the summer between sixth and seventh grade, and brushed the snow off with his hand until the words were visible:

Duffy, Laid to Rest in This Place, 1995.

That the dog had visited the night before, even if for only half a minute, served as confirmation that those we love are never really gone.

Finally, Dane knew what he had to do.

*   *   *

Ten minutes later, Dane returned to the house and told his parents everything.

"This girl, did Koda say what she looked like?" Ingrid asked.

"He said she was pretty," Dane said.

"Of course," Paul said.

"Pretty and gray," Dane added.

Paul and Ingrid exchanged glances. "What kind of state is he in, son? How is Koda coping?" Paul asked.

"Coping?" Dane said. "He's not coping. He's out of his mind. I've never seen him like this. Koda is the most unflappable person I've ever met, and now? He can't sleep, won't eat, just sits there... *waiting.*"

"You know, we'd be glad to work with him," Ingrid said.

Dane shook his head. Having Koda come to Lily Dale—to meet his parents and see Dane's humble beginnings—was out of the question.

"Well, maybe we could recommend someone," Paul said.

"Not from here," Dane said, "not from Lily Dale."

"What about that new guy people have been talking about?" Ingrid asked. "You know, the one down in St. Augustine. What was the man's name again?"

"Vooubasi?" Paul asked.

"Yes, that was it," Ingrid said. *"Vooubasi."*

LAS VEGAS, NEVADA
SEPTEMBER 14, 1935

Ulrich had been seeing Claudia twice a week for almost a year when she broke the news.

"I'm pregnant," Claudia blurted without warning.

"Fine, I will pay for an abortion," Ulrich said.

"Sorry, baby," Claudia said. "I'm Catholic. Abortion is out of the question."

"Adoption?"

Claudia shook her head. "No, we're going to have to find another option."

"What other option could there be?" Ulrich asked.

"Think, silly," Claudia said. *"Think!"*

"What? You want me to divorce my wife?" Ulrich asked.

"I told you, I'm Catholic," Claudia said. "Besides, a divorce would take too long."

"So what do you want me to do?" Ulrich asked.

"I want you to kill her," Claudia said.

"What?"

"You heard me," Claudia said.

"No, it is out of the question," Ulrich said. "There is no scenario under which I would kill Onyx."

"Ever? Really? Let me outline one for you," Claudia said. "How much do you owe The Owl now, four large?"

"The Owl? What does...?" Ulrich stammered.

"Let me put it another way, sweetie," Claudia said. "What do you think would happen if my daddy found out that—in addition to owing him $4,000—you also knocked-up his little girl?"

Bombs began exploding in Ulrich's skull.

"And not only did you knock me up, but you refused to do the honorable thing and marry me," Claudia said.

What was she saying?

"That's right, sweetie," Claudia said, taking a drag from her cigarette. "Faustino Spilatro is my father. And my three overly protective brothers—Fortunato, Flavio and Fabrizio—work for him, running his bar. Is that enough of a scenario for you?"

The Owl...

The Night Owl...

Oh, God.

The Night Owl was where Ulrich met Claudia for the first time. And what had The Owl said when he'd threatened him?

"You don't pay? I'll send my three sons to collect."

Ulrich thought he might throw up.

"It's not a big deal," Claudia said. "I've read up on all the ways you can do it, and the best is probably poison."

"Poison?" Ulrich repeated, as if in a state of shock.

"Yes," Claudia said.

"You want me to—?"

"Poison her, just like you would a rat."

SAVANNAH, GEORGIA
FEBRUARY 17, 1981

Born in China, educated in England, married in South Africa, and divorced in New Jersey, thirty-five-year old Cecelia Jaing's life had literally taken her to the four corners of the world. Now, as the youngest assistant district attorney in the history of Georgia, Cecelia finally felt like she was home.

She glanced up from her work and saw it was time to go.

The first time the death penalty had been carried out in the state of Georgia was the public hanging of Alice Riley from a large oak in the center of Wright Square in Savannah. Cecelia was sorry she'd missed it. She was also sorry she'd missed the five hundred hangings that followed.

What was interesting, Cecelia thought as she grabbed her purse and headed out the door, was that the people of Georgia felt that hanging someone by the neck until dead was perfectly fine for almost two hundred years. Then, suddenly, hanging was cruel and unusual punishment. There had to be a more reliable and humane method of putting someone to death.

Which led to the implementation of the electric chair.

Cecelia felt her heart begin to race as she drove past the prerequisite crowd of protestors, a common sight at state executions; so common, in fact, that an execution without one would somehow seem incomplete.

But it wasn't the protestors that bothered her. It was the fact that no matter how hard she tried she just couldn't get them to spell her name correctly. A protestor held up a cardboard sign that read: *"Chang the Clang is a Murderer!"* As in the sound a prison door made when being slammed. It was a nickname she enjoyed.

"It's not *Chang*, you moron—it's *Jaing. Jaing!*" How in the hell was she going to get elected governor if people couldn't find her on the ballot?

* * *

At 11:50 p.m., Cecelia watched as two prison guards strapped convicted wife-murderer Osvaldo Montezuma Sanchez into the electric chair. Lovingly referred to as New Sparky, the device had arrived at the state prison in Jackson just months earlier, having replaced Old Sparky.

Which had proved to be unreliable.

Assuming things went as planned, Cecelia would be in her car and heading back to Atlanta in less than twenty minutes.

Things didn't.

Osvaldo Sanchez was offered the opportunity to address the family and the other witnesses who had been invited to attend his execution.

He took it.

"I would like to recite a poem," Sanchez said.

A poem? Christ! Cecelia thought. What's next? Maybe they'll give him a guitar, and he can serenade the grief-stricken family. Then what, a few magic tricks?

Osvaldo Sanchez took a few steps forward, looked around the room—stopping for a second on each face—and started humming a tune.

Softly at first, so low Cecelia could barely hear him.

Ummm, ummm, ummm...

Then a bit louder:

Ummm, ummm, ummm, ummm...

It must be a prison tune of some kind, Cecelia thought.

Even louder now:

Ummm, ummm, ummm...

Osvaldo turned his head, looked Cecelia Jaing directly in the eye—gave a slight, almost imperceptible smile—and began to recite:

Brown bricks that are worn with age,
Metal bars that suppress the men's rage.
Initials and dates, scratched with a nail
So little to do when your life is a jail.

That which we eat, the tasteless mush,
"Lights out now! It's ten o'clock—hush!"
Then morning brings another harsh day
In the state of dread, in the state of GA.

Ummm, ummm, ummm...

The searing heat that starts by eight
So thick like water, it can suffocate.
The chains that clink, the chains that clank,
"Not tight enough? I'll give them a yank!"

The guard keeps watch, cradling his gun
Licking his lips, just hoping I'll run
Ain't nothin' the man would enjoy as well
As firing the shot that sends me to hell.

Ummm, ummm, ummm...

But the end of my time belongs not to him
For the light in my eyes when it finally dims
Won't lock on a guard or gaze at a gang
But rather the bitch, miss Cecelia Jaing.

"Jaing the Clang," with her long painted nails;
"Jaing the Clang," who controls all the rails.
"Jaing the Clang," who knew the true story,
But traded the facts for limelight and glory.

Ummm, ummm, ummm...

The "Jaing the Clang," in pursuit of career, who
Heard them say guilty then ordered a beer.
"Jaing the Clang," who believes she will win.
But just you wait—and think again.

*   *   *

The execution of Osvaldo Sanchez took twenty-nine minutes, during which time the innocent Hispanic man choked, jerked, snorted, drooled, and literally cooked to the horrified gasps of the assembled media and incessant sobs of family members.

"Do you think the governor will push to end executions in Georgia?" a reporter called out as Cecelia pushed her way through the protestors, who had grown from a small group of usual wing-nuts to an increasingly outraged mob.

"I have bigger fish to fry," Cecelia snapped.

Admittedly, it was not the most politically correct response under the circumstances, but one that guaranteed she'd be quoted on the front page of every newspaper in the country the next morning.

What would they be chanting if they knew that Sanchez was telling the truth? That someone had come forward years earlier and provided incontrovertible evidence that proved Osvaldo Sanchez could not possibly have committed the crime, and Cecelia had decided to ignore it.

Cecelia knew that making the information public would have called her professionalism into question—*which was out of the question*—even though doing so would save an innocent man's life.

In any case, Sanchez was off her to-do list. Now, it was time to turn her full attention to a new case, one that involved the disappearance of a local girl named Juniper Cole, who'd been abducted on the night of her senior prom.

Though the body had never been found, there was enough evidence to put the scum in the same chair Osvaldo Sanchez's limp body was being pulled from at that very minute.

What was the guy's name? Oh, yeah, that's right.

It was Wyatt.

Wyatt Scrogger.

DESOTO, MISSOURI
MARCH 26, 1925

Our Lady of the Open Arms was larger than Katherine had expected, but otherwise it was like every orphanage she'd ever seen; a central, brown-brick building with an attached chapel, rectory, and infirmary, all of which were surrounded by a series of smaller buildings that had been added over the years.

Unlike many of the other missions God had sent Katherine on, getting there was easy.

Over the previous twelve years, Katherine had been sent to a variety of places—some thousands of miles from her home in St. Louis. This was just forty-seven miles to the south.

The morning after the tornado vision, Katherine turned on the radio and heard the news. An enormous twister had crossed the Mississippi River at 2:33 p.m. the previous afternoon, ripping through the town of Gorham and obliterating everything that stood in its path, taking thirty-four lives in less than five minutes. Moving next in a north-easterly direction at an average speed of sixty-two miles per hour, the monster twister set its sights on Murphysboro, Illinois, not too far from the Illinois-Missouri state line.

Fifty minutes later, 695 lives would be lost, and two thousand more seriously injured.

Thomas Bilazzo and his wife, Luisa, were among the dead, of that much Katherine was certain. Why would God have sent her to an orphanage otherwise? Beyond that, she had no idea what her mission was. Certainly God didn't want her to adopt the boy? Then again...

"God doesn't send you out for eggs unless he wants you to make an omelet," Katherine's mother used to say when she would share the details of her latest vision.

Her father, on the other hand, wanted nothing to do with God or his daughter's visions. *"No God of mine would have taken you from us,"* he would say. *"Six years, in torment, wondering if you were alive or dead, why would any God do that to a parent?"*

That God had returned Katherine home to them—alive—made no difference.

Katherine entered the large front doors of the orphanage and found the office.

"I'm here about Tommy Bilazzo," Katherine said.

The nun at the desk checked a printed list. "I will summon Sister Mary Margaret," the nun said. "It may be a while. There are chairs in the hallway, if you'd like to take a seat."

Katherine couldn't sit.

She was filled with energy, as if an electric charge had been placed within her. It was always the way she felt when God sent her to do His work on Earth.

To fill the time, Katherine walked the halls of the large building, which looked to have been built sometime in the mid-1800s.

In the distance, she could hear the sound of children singing.

Ding dong, bell, the pussy is in the well.
Who put her in? Little Johnny Flynn.
Who pulled her out? Little Tommy Stout.
What a naughty boy was that,
To try to drown poor pussy cat,
Who ne'er did him the slightest harm
But kill all the mice in the farmer's barn.

It was a song Katherine knew all too well. She'd been forced to sing the tune again and again in Obedience Everhardt's cellar—the old woman sitting across from her in a rocking chair, doing her knitting—Katherine never knowing if she was singing it for the last time.

Enough of that, Katherine thought.

Thoughts of her time in that place had stopped making her cry long ago. The only thing left now was the desire to do God's work in whatever form that work might take.

As she glanced along the wall, a picture caught her eye...

It was a black-and-white framed photograph of a nun and an older woman with a long gray ponytail standing in front of the orphanage.

Suddenly the words to the second verse of the song entered Katherine's mind without even having to think:

> *Ding dong bell, the pussy is in the well.*
> *Who took her there? Little Johnny Hare.*
> *Who'll bring her in? Little Tommy Thin.*
> *What a jolly boy was that,*
> *To get some milk for pussy cat,*
> *Who ne'er did any harm,*
> *But play with the mice in his father's barn.*

Katherine took a step closer, studied the old woman's face. It was considerably older than she'd remembered—more wrinkles, the skin sagging around her chin—but there was no doubt.

It was Obedience Everhardt.

Maybe God had not brought her here to adopt Tommy Bilazzo, Katherine thought. Maybe he'd brought her here to kill Obedience.

Katherine had waited for over twenty years for this moment to arrive, and now—completely unexpectedly—here it was. What would she say if she came face to face with Obedience? What would she do to her if she was provided the gift of ten minutes alone in a room with her? Did she have the courage?

The fantasy in Katherine's imagination was interrupted by the sound of footsteps echoing from the end of the corridor.

"I am Sister Mary Margaret," the nun said as she approached. Katherine immediately recognized her as the same nun in the photograph on the wall. "I understand you are inquiring about one of our new arrivals, Tommy Bilazzo?"

"The woman with you in this picture," Katherine said, "This is you, correct?"

The nun glanced at the photo. "And you are...?"

"I'm the one who got away," Katherine said.

"Got away?" Sister Mary Margaret repeated. "I'm quite certain I don't understand."

"Do you know where she is?" Katherine asked.

Sister Mary Margaret nodded and said, "Yes."

Katherine's heart skipped a beat.

"She's exactly where we buried her," the nun said.

"She's dead?"

"Quite dead," Sister Mary Margaret said. "Hanging yourself with a rope will tend to do that to you."

The nun's words hit Katherine with such force the air was knocked from her lungs, making it hard for her to breathe. "When?" Katherine finally managed.

"Day before yesterday," Sister Mary Margaret said.

Katherine couldn't understand it. Why would God bring her to where Obedience was after all these years, only to have her get there two days too late to do anything about it? "I don't... I don't... Why?" Katherine said leaning against the wall to steady herself.

Sister Mary Margaret reached out and grabbed Katherine's arm, holding her upright. "Come, child, come with me," the nun said soothingly.

* * *

Katherine and Sister Mary Margaret sat in the back pew of the chapel, a large white statue of Saint Therese of Lisieux looking down on them.

"I imagine I should be happy," Katherine said, "knowing it is finally finished and in God's hands."

"But you're not," Sister Mary Margaret said.

"No. All I feel is emptiness, like I've been cheated."

"Cheated by God?" the nun asked.

"Yes," Katherine said. "That He didn't trust me."

"Trust you? To do what? To take care of it yourself?"

Katherine paused, knowing how bad it would sound if she told the truth. "Yes," she said anyway.

"Have you ever considered doing God's work, Katherine?" the nun asked finally.

"I thought I was," Katherine said.

"Yes, but I mean formally. Officially," Sister Mary Margaret said.

"You mean...?"

"Yes," Sister Mary Margaret said. "I mean, have you ever considered joining the convent?"

"It is not important to know what fate awaits
you beyond the living plane. All that **matters**
is that you know there is a 'there' there."

*The 31 Immutable Matters
of Life & Death*

SNEAK PREVIEW
from
Book Two

DESOTO, MISSOURI
JANUARY 20, 1935

Sister Mary Margaret dipped her hand into the tub. Still not hot enough, she thought, then turned the knob a bit more to the right. Taking a second bath on the same day was strictly forbidden as water consumption needed to be kept to a minimum.

Sister Mary Margaret went to her secret hiding place next, where she kept her cigarettes and a box of wooden matches— also against the orphanage's strict rules. She withdrew a single unfiltered Old Gold, her first choice not because of the taste or quality of the tobacco, but because the package pictured a woman who looked unrestricted, like she was someone who enjoyed doing what she wanted, whenever she wanted.

Next in the nightly routine was music, which wasn't forbidden so much as frowned upon, as Father Fanning believed evening hours in one's room were for silent prayers.

Fanning was an idiot.

Sister Katherine was another story. Sharp as a whip, she turned out to be. Always watching, always aware. Perhaps convincing the woman to join the convent ten years earlier had been a mistake. Perhaps she'd have to be dealt with.

Sister Mary Margaret's current choice of music after a long day dealing with cackling young girls and disgusting little boys was *Das Veilchen vom Montmarte,* a three-act operetta by Hungarian composer Emmerich Kálmán. Listening to the likes of Benny Goodman and Al Jolson was intolerable once one had experienced Kálmán, she thought.

She placed the needle on the record and let her robe drop to the floor, exposing her overweight fifty-nine-year-old body to the cool air of the rectory. She climbed in the tub, lit her cigarette, and closed her eyes, letting the hot water run to keep the tub the perfect temperature.

Father Fanning thinks he runs this place, Sister Mary Margaret mused, sucking in a lung-full of smoke and blowing a blue cloud toward the ceiling. In truth, she made the place work, through unbending rules, harsh discipline and—when necessary—glorious, cleansing pain.

* * *

On the other side of the paper-thin wall that separated the rooms in the rectory, Sister Katherine Keane knelt on a folded towel at the edge of her bed, reading from the Bible she received as a gift from her parents on her thirteenth birthday—a birthday she would not have seen without the enormous sacrifice made by a St. Louis police detective.

Next door the music began to play as it did every night, which didn't bother Katherine as much as the fact that Father Fanning would do nothing to curb Sister Mary Margaret's vices.

Of course, after ten years now as a sister at Our Lady of the Open Arms, she was used to all kinds of things, many of them in direct contradiction to the word of God and the teachings of the Bible.

Katherine turned to Romans 12:19 and read: *"Beloved, never avenge yourselves, but leave it to the wrath of God, for it is written, 'Vengeance is mine, I will repay, says the Lord.'"*

But she knew the scripture had been written for others, not her. For on that day—when Detective Boyd exchanged his life for hers—Katherine stood naked before God, basking in His light as God shared His vision for her:

"You are my eyes and ears on earth, Katherine, and it is through your eyes that I shall see the doers of evil and through your hand that I shall extract my vengeance."

And then God returned Katherine to her body so she could take her place as a foot soldier in the Army of the Lord, and He took Detective Stormy Boyd in her place. She was good and clean and pure, nothing like Sister Mary Margaret in the next room, smoking her cigarettes and playing her sinful music. And claiming to love the children? *Please.*

The old nun's actions would not go unseen, unnoticed, or unrecorded—because Sister Katherine Keane was watching.

And God was watching through her.

Katherine finished saying her prayers, returned the Bible to its proper place under her pillow, and retrieved the latest copy of *True Detective* magazine from its hiding spot under the mattress. It was the one guilty pleasure she allowed herself before turning in each evening.

Katherine went to the sink to remove the makeup she wore to cover the scar that ran through her upper and lower lip. Yes, makeup was against the rules, too.

But she knew God would understand.

SAVANNAH, GEORGIA
JUNE 2, 1982

So, Mr. Scrogger," Assistant District Attorney Cecelia Jaing began. "If I understand the primary theme of your defense, you were—in your own words—'*too drunk to have killed anyone.*' Is that a fair summary?"

"I'd had a few beers," Wyatt muttered.

"A few as in three? Four?"

"I'm not sure."

"Ten? Twelve?" Cecelia pushed.

"Yeah, probably," Wyatt said.

"And is it your testimony that the dozen-plus beers you had over the course of the evening were consumed at only two bars, Pinkie Masters and the Cosmos Club?"

"Yes."

"And you stopped at no other establishments that evening, is that correct?"

"Yes, that's correct," Wyatt said.

"I have no more questions for this witness, Your Honor," Cecelia said. A few whispers flew around the stunned courtroom as the cross-examination of Wyatt Scrogger was expected to last several days.

Wyatt shrugged, relieved at having been dismissed so quickly. But no sooner had Wyatt returned to his seat at the defense table than Cecelia Jaing dropped the bomb.

"The prosecution calls Ms. Marjorie Schrump to the stand," Cecelia announced.

The defense attorney scanned the witness list and rose to his feet. "Objection, Your Honor. There is no such person on the prosecution's witness list."

"That's because Ms. Schrump is a rebuttal witness for the purposes of impeachment," Cecelia said.

"Very well," the judge said.

Marjorie Schrump was sworn in and took the stand.

"Ms. Schrump, can you tell the court where you were on the evening of June 2 and early morning of June 3, 1979.

"Yes, I was at the Forsyth Park Hotel."

"Directly across from Forsyth Park?" Cecelia prompted.

"Yes, that's it," Schrump said.

"And in what capacity were you there?"

"I was acting as a chaperone for Savannah High School, which was holding its senior prom there that evening," Schrump continued.

"And on that evening did you see the defendant in this case there in the hotel?"

"Yes, I did."

Gasps.

"And at what time did you see the defendant in the hotel?" Cecelia asked.

"Somewhere between 12:10 a.m. and 12:30 a.m.," Schrump said.

"How can you be so certain what time it was?"

"Because my duties as chaperone ended promptly at midnight, and several of the other chaperones and I went over to the bar for a well-deserved glass of Chardonnay. You have no idea what it's like to watch over a group of two hundred horny teenagers," Schrump said.

Giggles from the gallery.

"And did you simply see Mr. Scrogger at the hotel that evening? Or did you happen to come in contact with him?"

"We came in contact with one another."

"Could you please describe the nature of this contact?" Cecelia prompted.

"Yes. He approached me and asked me a question."

"A question?" Cecelia repeated for dramatic effect. "And what was the question he asked?"

"He asked me if I knew where the bathrooms were."

"Is that all? Did he ask you anything else?"

"Yes," the woman said. "He asked me if I knew where he could find Juniper Cole."

ST. AUGUSTINE, FLORIDA
FEBRUARY 22, 2010

When Koda Mulvaney's jet touched down in Orlando, he convinced Tank—his father's Samoan limo driver and bodyguard—to drive him to his meeting with Vooubasi in St. Augustine, ninety miles away.

Dane was already waiting in the lobby of the Casa Monica hotel when they arrived. He'd flown in from New York earlier that day.

"How'd you talk Koda into this?" Tank asked as he reached out to give Dane a bone-crushing handshake. Tank was wide and strong, having played left tackle—protecting quarterback Bruce Mulvaney's blind-side—for three seasons as a Georgia Bulldog—which was appropriate since Tank actually resembled a bulldog.

"So he told you about the girl?" Dane asked.

"Yeah. Every girl in the world wants the kid and what does he do? He falls for the one chick he can't have."

Dane laughed. Koda didn't.

"I haven't fallen for her," Koda said flatly. "I just want to understand what's going on."

"We're supposed to meet with Vooubasi at six," Dane said.

Koda glanced at his watch. "Let's get checked in, then meet in the bar at 5:30, okay?"

"Checked in?" Tank asked.

"Yeah, we're staying the night," Koda said.

"I'm gonna have to tell your old man I'm not coming back tonight," Tank said. "You cool with that?"

Koda nodded. "Just don't tell him why we're here, okay?"

"Don't worry. I'll tell him you and Dane are gonna go clubbing, and I'm staying to keep you out of trouble."

* * *

A young Asian woman met Dane, Koda, and Tank at the door to Vooubasi's suite and ushered them into the sitting area where they found the psychic medium seated on a sofa in the corner of the room.

Vooubasi was a small man, probably no more than five-foot-five or six at best. He was dark as a raisin left too long in the midday sun, with a mass of wavy black and gray hair that hung well past his shoulders, and wore what appeared to be a 1960s Beatles-era Nehru jacket. And then there were his laughably oversized platform shoes.

"I am Vooubasi," the small man said in a strong Indian accent, suggesting he was raised in either India or Pakistan. "You have met my assistant, Xiao-Xing. She will also be participating in this evening's event."

"Event?" Dane asked.

"Yes," Vooubasi said, "during the séance."

"The séance?" Koda repeated.

"When we spoke by phone, I asked you what you wanted to achieve by meeting," Vooubasi said in a calm tone. "If my memory serves me, you said you wanted to reach someone on the other side—a girl, I believe—correct?"

"Yes, but I didn't realize—"

"I have been doing this for many years, Mr. Mulvaney," Vooubasi continued. "A séance is the vehicle to achieve your desires."

"There is the small issue of payment and the release," Xiao-Xing briefly stepped forward to explain.

"Release?" Tank said. "Release for what?"

"Standard boilerplate stuff," Vooubasi explained with a wave of his brown hand, as if he were shooing away a fly. "A standard protection in case anyone should have a heart attack or get cut by flying glass."

"Seriously?" Dane asked. He'd sat in on many séances in his younger years in Lily Dale but had never witnessed anything flying around the room, except for the occasional tambourine.

Vooubasi shrugged his frail shoulders. "Anything is possible when one is dealing with the other side."

"Fine, let's just get on with it," Koda said, writing Vooubasi a check for $10,000—an amount he knew he was currently unable to cover—glanced quickly at the release, and scribbled his signature at the bottom.

"Mr. Vooubasi will be spending the next few hours in deep meditation as a means of preparation," Xiao-Xing said. "May I suggest you return to your rooms and get proper rest. Return here at 11:45 p.m., at which time I will give everyone their instructions."

DESOTO, MISSOURI
APRIL 17, 1935

Thirteen-year-old Declan Mulvaney was being punished for speaking out of turn.

Sister Mary Margaret instructed the boy to stand behind a large upright piano in the corner of the classroom, where he now found himself watching a large black spider spinning its web less than three inches from his face.

When the class bell rang, Sister Mary Margaret—whom the children shortened to Sister "Mar Mar" behind her back—told Declan to stay behind. Once they were alone, she pulled a wooden ruler from her desk drawer.

"You are a special boy, Declan Mulvaney," Sister Mary Margaret said. "But I have come to learn that the special boys require extra-special reminders to behave in class. Hold out your hand, please."

Declan extended his arm, opening his hand in front of Mar Mar's face. In his open palm was the crushed spider.

Sister Mary Margaret did not scare easily, but the unexpected sight of the large arachnid caught her off guard and she took an involuntary step backward. Regaining her composure, she said, "Turn your palm down, Declan, knuckles up."

"No," Declan said.

"Declan Mulvaney, you will do as I say."

"No," Declan said again.

Sister Mary Margaret and Declan locked eyes. Neither of them blinked. Sister Mary Margaret finally spoke. "Very well, Mr. Mulvaney, have it your way. But don't bother going to dinner with the others this evening. There will be none for you."

Declan turned his hand over, dropped the dead spider at Mar Mar's feet and walked out of the room.

* * *

Later, after lights out, ten-year-old Tommy Bilazzo made his way in the darkness to Declan's bunk on the other side of the boy's dormitory. Like virtually every kid at Open Arms, Tommy admired Declan for his brash attitude and refusal to submit to every rule imposed at the institution they were forced to call home.

Tommy was taking a risk of his own now.

"I copped some bread for you. It was all I could get," Tommy said, producing a hunk of sourdough from his pocket.

Declan nodded and took the bread from Tommy Bilazzo's hand.

Tommy was three years younger than Declan—but so big that the two boys looked like they were the same age. He'd arrived at the Open Arms three years after Declan, after his mother and father perished in the Tri-state tornado of 1925. Of course, everyone at the orphanage had such a story—it was, after all, how each of them had come to be there in the first place.

"What was it like being back there?" Tommy asked. "Alone, behind the piano, I mean."

"I wasn't alone. There was a big black spider to keep me company," Declan said taking a bite from the bread.

"I don't like spiders much," Tommy replied.

"Me neither. That's why I killed it," Declan said.

"Why'd you do that?" Tommy asked. "It wasn't the spider's fault Sister Mar Mar stuck you back there."

"He was in my face," Declan said. "Anything that gets in my face dies."

Declan Mulvaney had a well-earned reputation at the orphanage as a brawler, one of the boys not to be messed with. Tommy Bilazzo had the exact opposite reputation. Though Tommy was big enough to pummel just about anyone he wanted, he'd never been in a fight and hoped he'd never have to.

Though Declan Mulvaney and Tommy Bilazzo had grown up in the same place, under the same conditions, the two boys could not have been more different.

Declan reached down and pulled a copy of *Boy's Life* magazine from under his mattress.

"Where'd you get that?" Tommy asked.

"I copped it from Father Fanning's office," Declan said as he flipped through the magazine. "He won't miss it. He's got a whole stack of 'em." Declan found the page he was looking for and held it open for Tommy to see.

"What is it?" Tommy asked, straining to see the picture in the darkened room.

"That, my friend, is a Boeing Vultee eight-passenger with an airspeed of 230 miles an hour and a fourteen-cylinder engine," Declan said. "I'm gonna own one someday. What about you?"

"Own a plane?" Tommy Bilazzo repeated.

"Yeah, why not?"

"I dunno," Tommy said with a shrug of his shoulders. "Never thought about it."

"Here, take the magazine and read up on it," Declan said.

Tommy took the magazine back to his bunk, though neither the magazine nor the airplane meant much to him. What mattered most was that Declan Mulvaney—the coolest kid in the entire orphanage—had just called him his friend.

LAS VEGAS, NEVADA
OCTOBER 1, 1935

Give her the whole box of poison if you have to," Claudia said after Ulrich updated her on Onyx's condition.

Ulrich knew he couldn't put more in her food than he had already, or Onyx would know for sure. So he switched to other poisons. First he tried arsenic, then cyanide, then Lysol—then mercury, laundry detergent, sulfur, hemlock, analine dye, pyrethrum, and Jamaica ginger.

Nothing worked.

Each time Ulrich switched to a different poison, Onyx was unaffected for a few days, then she'd get violently ill. And just when it seemed she coud not go on another minute, she'd recover somehow.

Ulrich was out-of-his-mind perplexed. He'd given her more poison than any human should be able to survive. Damn it, why wouldn't she die?

After a full month had passed, Claudia was apoplectic.

"I don't care what you have to do, strangle her or throw her in front of a train, but Onyx is either dead by tomorrow or I will tell my daddy—The Owl—everything."

* * *

Ulrich waited until one o'clock in the morning to walk over to the train station where he stole an unlocked Chrysler. Then he drove down Fremont and parked across from The Apache. On the front car seat next to him was a two-foot length of rope and a pair of leather gloves.

Onyx would be done with her final set around two.

Admittedly, he hadn't taken Onyx seriously when she'd told him she was going to start singing; after all, he'd never heard her sing a note before that time. Now Ulrich could see Onyx on stage through the large front windows of The Apache from where he was parked. The silky-smooth strains of her voice drifted out onto Fremont Street.

He sat there listening as Onyx worked her way through her set list... "Smoke Gets in Your Eyes"... "All of Me"... "I've Got the World On a String"... "Try a Little Tenderness"... wrapping with her favorite song of all, "Moonlight Bay."

Suddenly Ulrich found himself thinking about the first day he'd met Onyx near the Tchefuncte River Lighthouse on the banks of Lake Ponchartrain and how beautiful she looked in the mid-day sunlight. It was as if a fever broke. *What in the hell was he doing?*

Ulrich put the car in drive, did a U-turn on Fremont and took a right on Ogden toward The Night Owl.

He didn't have to kill Onyx.

He could kill Claudia!

*   *   *

Ulrich turned off the headlamps of the stolen Chrysler and pulled into the rear lot behind The Night Owl saloon.

Ulrich looked at his watch. It was ten minutes after two in the morning, and he knew that Claudia would be coming out any minute. He pulled on the leather gloves, grabbed the rope and walked in the darkness to the rear door of the building, near the bottom of the stairs.

Ten minutes passed and still no Claudia. Ulrich took a few steps to his left and peered through the window into the club. Claudia was on her hands and knees, pulling on a metal ring and lifting up a door that was hidden in the floor. Claudia placed a large stack of bills into the hiding spot, lowered the door and repositioned a small rug over the area.

Ulrich made his way back to the car with another change in plan. Don't murder Onyx *or* Claudia; just steal the money and go! That would serve everyone right. Surely there was a woman out there who'd truly appreciate him.

Ulrich waited for Claudia to lock the door and leave. With no one in sight, Ulrich punched the glass window with his gloved fist, reached in and undid the lock. He quickly stepped inside and went to the spot.

Ulrich pulled the rug back, pulled on the metal ring and gasped. The secret compartment didn't have that day's receipts—it must have had a month's worth. There was so much money he couldn't hold it all and searched around for a bag to carry it in.

I have just pulled off the heist of the century, Ulrich thought as he made his way to the door, *and from the Spilatros no less!*

Then, Ulrich heard a noise from behind him.

Ulrich turned to see Flavio Spilatro—one of the brothers—standing behind him. Having had too much to drink, as usual, Flavio had passed out in the rear booth of the saloon. Now he'd finally come to.

"Who in the hell are you?" Flavio asked, slurring his words.

The question was apparently rhetorical since he did not wait for an answer and rushed at Ulrich like a drunken football player. Ulrich took a step to the left and watched as Flavio grabbed at thin air and went tumbling down the stairs—promptly breaking his neck.

Ulrich peered down the stairs.

There was no movement.

Christ.

Stealing money from the mob was bad enough, but killing a mob boss's son?

Ulrich ran from the bar, climbed in the car, and began pounding his fists on the steering wheel. "Damn it!" he yelled. How could things have gone so bad so quickly? Why did the world have it out for him?

Ulrich looked at his watch. It was almost three in the morning. He needed to get home, get packed, get Onyx, and get out of town.

*   *   *

Though Ulrich told Onyx not to go to the doctor under the guise of their not being able to afford it, she'd gone anyway.

Now, almost a week later, the doctor who'd seen Onyx received the detailed report for the blood he'd drawn and couldn't believe what he was reading.

Poison.

More accurately, *poisons.*

And in such large quantities no human could survive with them in his or her bloodstream.

He dialed the telephone number of the patient—a woman named Onyx Webb—written on her paperwork. It turned out to be a work number for a place called The Apache.

The manager at The Apache informed the doctor that Ms. Webb had failed to show for her last three work shifts and had been fired. No, they did not have any forwarding information.

The doctor hung up the phone, upset that he was unable to warn the woman that someone close to her clearly wanted her dead.

The tests did not lie.

Onyx Webb was being poisoned.

And as if that were not enough, she was pregnant. Whoever was poisoning the woman was not only killing her but also poisoning her baby.

GET ENTANGLED

www.OnyxWebb.com

The story continues in
Onyx Webb: Book Two.
In the meantime, we'd honored
if you wrote a review.

About Diandra Archer...

With two previous #1 Amazon bestsellers to their credit, Richard Fenton & Andrea Waltz—*writing as Diandra Archer*—have had a burning desire to create a paranormal ghost series for as long as they can remember.

Then, one day while walking around Lake Eola in the heart of downtown Orlando, the right idea struck. "The minute we came up with Onyx Webb—a ghost that would give anything for one more day of life, watching in torment while the living sleep-walk through life like ghosts—we knew we had it," Andrea says.

"The story lines for the major characters were created within a matter of days," Richard adds. "But getting a collection of complex characters from mind to page—in a 10-book saga that spans more than a century, in an easy-to-consume format—was another matter entirely."

Andrea Waltz & Richard Fenton

When not traveling, Richard & Andrea can be found in Orlando, Florida—typing as fast as they can—with their *ghost cat*, Courage, at their feet.